MXAC

D1269699

Murda Was the Case

Lock Down Publications and

Ca$h Presents

Murda Was the Case

A Novel by *Elijah R. Freeman*

Lock Down Publications
Po Box 944
Stockbridge, Ga 30281

Visit our website
www.lockdownpublications.com

First Edition September 2021
Printed in the United States of America

Lock Down Publications
Like our page on Facebook: Lock Down Publications @
www.facebook.com/lockdownpublications.ldp

Book interior design by: **Shawn Walker**
Edited by: **Shamika Smith**

Stay Connected with Us!

Text **LOCKDOWN** to 22828 to stay up-to-date with new releases, sneak peaks, contests and more…

Thank you.

Submission Guideline.

Submit the first three chapters of your completed manuscript to ldpsubmissions@gmail.com, subject line: Your book's title. The manuscript must be in a .doc file and sent as an attachment. The document should be in Times New Roman, double-spaced and in size 12 font. Also, provide your synopsis and full contact information. If sending multiple submissions, they must each be in a separate email.

Have a story but no way to send it electronically? You can still submit to LDP/Ca$h Presents. Send in the first three chapters, written or typed, of your completed manuscript to:

LDP: Submissions Dept
Po Box 944
Stockbridge, Ga 30281

DO NOT send original manuscript. Must be a duplicate.

Provide your synopsis and a cover letter containing your full contact information.

Thanks for considering LDP and Ca$h Presents.

CHAPTER 1

J-Bo took a deep breath, stroking the back of his head. "Listen, Ken. We've been sittin' here long enough, bruh. All you gotta do is reach out to da punk-ass bitch and tell her you got fifty thousand for her not to testify."

J-Bo's frustration was clear. Charged with a number of Georgia's Seven Deadly Sins, he and his lil' cousin, Flip, had been sitting in the county jail for almost a year now, and he needed his best friend to move faster.

"If she agrees to meet you…" J-Bo's voice trailed off, conscious of his surroundings, aware now of the visitation officer's casual approach. A baby began crying a few seats down from them.

"Everything alright here, fellers?" He was a short, rounded Caucasian with a bald head and almost red skin.

"Yea," J-Bo stubbornly retorted, waving him off. He knew officer Cloth was racist from prior altercations, the latest of which was him putting a black guy in handcuffs and beating him for stealing an extra sack lunch. J-Bo hated how C.O.'s acted as though money for food was coming out of their pockets.

"I hate that crack, shawty."

Ken wasn't a fan of unnecessary jargon, jokes, or causal talk. He was a muscle-bound, handsome guy, standing at six-two, weighing in at two-hundred and ten pounds with thick dreads that fell just past his shoulders. And with a single word, "Continue," his natural disposition was clear with him wanting to hear nothing more than J-Bo's proposal.

"Right." J-Bo lowered his tone and glanced over his shoulder for potential eavesdroppers. "When she meets with you, you know what ta do."

“And if she agrees to deal but doesn’t want to meet?” Ken was quick to cover the bases.

“Never mind the fact I have no way of getting in touch with her.”

J-Bo glanced over his shoulder again, keeping his voice low. “If she don’t wanna meet, then fuck it. Just send da money. She got a sister- a fine-ass yellow bone named Nae. I went to high school wit' her.” He scratched an itch in his nappy twists, those which were only now beginning to lock. He smiled, showing his chipped tooth. J-Bo was 5’7” and barely made one-hundred and sixty pounds in weight. Even so, he was a major player in YoungBoss. “Get in good with her until she brings you around Diamond's dusty ass.”

Ken sat contemplatively silent as J-Bo rambled on, offering various suggestions for him to carry out the act. “I’m not with all that lovey-dovey shit,” he said at last, “but to free my brother, I'll get it done.”

“Yea,” J-Bo said. “Plus, she loves dread heads.” J-Bo laughed, nearly bringing a smile to Ken's lips. That is until Officer Cloth ruined the moment.

“This damned visit is over!” He was speed walking towards J-Bo. Mugging the approaching officer, Ken quickly stood to his feet. He didn’t need J-Bo to tell him the red-neck honkey was racist. He could smell it on him, and he wanted him to know it could pop here and now.

Cloth tapped J-Bo's shoulder, a signal for him to rise in order to be placed in handcuffs. “Fuck you jumping up like you’re gonna do something for, boy!” One by one, J-Bo’s wrists were cuffed, and several officers alerted by Cloth's outburst came to surround Ken in their fellow officer's defense, Ken hardly flinched.

“Is there a problem, sir?” the question came from a middle-aged, black sergeant.

Cloth turned to escort J-Bo away, but J-Bo planted his feet, calling back to his friend. Ken caught his eye between the surrounding officers, and J-Bo shook his head. "Don't give these folks a reason, shawty, you on a mission."

****

Back in the dorm, J-Bo took the stairs by twos on the way to his cell. He and Flip were biological cousins and co-defendants on a triple homicide case.

"What up, cuz?" Flip popped the question the moment his cousin crossed the threshold. "Erthang straight?"

J-Bo sat resignedly down on his bed. "Yea, Ken gon' handle it."

Flip took a deep breath, scratching the back of his head. J-Bo's words were clear, but his actions said there was more. Flip knew Ken to be a man of his word. "So, what you stressin' for?"

"I just don't understand why this monkey-ass bitch wanna testify on us," J-Bo vented. "I mean, she don't know us from a can of paint. Dumb bitch don't even know I'm finna have her ass touched," he vented, brows creased in confusion. "I mean, what you gettin' off of helpin' da state anyway?" He clenched his fist, angry at the thought of a living witness.

"Just a punk-bitch tryna be a good Samaritan." Flip removed a small bag of tobacco he had ducked off in his sock, tore a small rectangle size piece of paper from the Bible, and began rolling a cigarette. "Quit trippin', cuz. Ken gon' handle dat. We gon' be back out there before you know it, livin' dat life again." With two razor blades and two AA batteries, he set fire to the cigarette, inhaling deep. "You know what I be thinkin' bout doe, cuz?"

"What?"

"What da hell was ole girl doin' out there that night anyway?"

"Prolly gettin' butt-fucked," J-Bo teased.

Together they laugh at a joke that was closer to the truth than they both knew.

****

ELEVEN MONTHS AGO

"Aw shit, Daddy," Diamond moaned. She was bent over in the driver's seat of her car with her boyfriend, Garrett, delivering alternating strokes deep into her ass and her pussy. They were parked behind an abandoned building that was once a Wal-Mart. The two had been on the way home from a late dinner when Garrett, having had enough of their flirtatious exchange, suggested they find a spot to handle the business. Several abandoned cars were present. Other than the sounds of traffic from one of the busiest interstates in Georgia above which they were parked, the two were all alone in their passion. A black Yukon appeared, coming to a stop twenty feet away from them. Two men got out and looked cautiously about.

"Baby, wait," Diamond protested. "Don't you see them niggas?"

Garrett could care less, positioned as he was between the console and the driver's seat. He was aware of the SUV and the two men, but his concern was for the ass he was in and the nut he was about to bust. The newcomers seemed to be about their own business, and so was he.

One of the shadowed figures popped the trunk. Two bound figures were snatched from the rear of the SUV and thrown face down to the pavement. They were young, male and female, the latter of which was either pudgy or pregnant.

"Oh, god!" Diamond exclaimed. "Garrett, stop!"

Near to climax, Garrett did otherwise, pleading for her to wait a second longer, his grip tight on her waist with increasingly quick strokes.

"No!" Diamond twisted away, causing him to slip out of her ass.

"Goddamn, Diamond!" he snapped. "Mind yo fuckin' business. They ain't fuckin' wit us. Come on."

She was quick to pull her leggings in place, annoyed with his selfish act for sex under the circumstances. Garrett sucked his teeth, and she lowered the driver-side window a few inches to hear as she peered into the night at the armed figures.

"Please, my nigga," the boy begged, spitting blood between sobs.

"The girl looks pregnant," Diamond whispered, "and the boy might be her baby daddy."

The taller of the two figures moved to squat next to the boy on the ground. "I'm going to ask you one more time. Where is my money?"

"I told you already," the boy replied. "I spent it."

The taller figure glanced around. The boy did, likewise, taking in the dark lot, the surrounding trees, and stripped cars. There was no one to call and no one to hear them scream. Fate was clear; they were going to die here tonight. He looked to his girlfriend, who was crying audibly and offering prayers to a God he wasn't sure existed. The certainty of which he would soon know. "Please, bra. Just give me two weeks, and I'll have it all back to you."

The tall figure shook his head, releasing a deep sigh.

Desperate now, the boy wiggled onto his back and took a second look at his praying girlfriend. "She's pregnant and had nothing to do with it. Please let her go."

The taller guy stood and nodded at his partner.

"Let me get this straight," the second male spoke from his position near the praying girl. "Yo dumb-ass break in our spot and steal a quarter-mill. Then you spend it up and go get your hoe pregnant like shit's sweet? Sounds to me like an expensive abortion and funeral."

"Bruh, please!" the boy cried, but his plea fell on deaf ears as the second guy pulled a Glock .40 off his waist and sent two rounds into the girl. One in the back, one in the dome. The first guy followed suit with shots from his .45, sending four slugs into the teen's torso.

Diamond fell away from the window with a startled scream, silenced by Garret's hand covering her mouth. A witness to a murder, and they would suffer a similar fate if they were discovered.

The taller one of the shadow figures stood, glancing about the empty lot.

"What?" the second male asked, taking a look around as well.

The tall figure eyed the abandoned cars twenty feet away. Satisfied that he was just trippin', he shook it off. "Nothing. Let's get the fuck on. The last thing we need is to get spotted on the scene."

"Right."

They jogged to the truck, hopped in, cranked up, and pulled off.

Diamond snatched her cellphone from the floor and typed in the Yukon's license plate and started dialing 911 to report the incident as the suspects disappeared into the night.

"Baby, what are you doing?"

"What you think?" Diamond shot back.

"Baby," Garrett cautioned, "maybe, we should mind our own business."

Diamond placed the phone to her ear. "You can, but I'm calling that shit in."

****

"Baby," Garrett stated for the thousandth time, dating back from the beginning of this ordeal. "I don't think you should testify on those guys." They were in a private hotel, alone together in bed that had been provided by the state as part of Georgia's Witness Protection program. "Look at us; we've been living in here for almost a year now. We got security around this bitch 24/7- and it's not even our business, Diamond."

With the D.A having disclosed the details of the case, Diamond just couldn't let it go. "Those were kids; Seventeen years old, Garrett. Their families need justice."

She met his gaze from where she sat across from him. He was caught by how good she looked in nothing but pink boy shorts and a bra to match. However, he couldn't allow himself to be distracted.

"But you don't even know why they were killed, Diamond. Just stay in yo own fuckin' lane, damn!" He rose from the bed, disgusted with her and himself as well. He pointed a finger in her face and spoke through clenched teeth. "Call the D.A and tell him you want out so we can move on with our lives."

"No!" She smacked his hand from her face.

"Well, I am. I'm done with this shit!"

Garret went to the closet for the small backpack that he'd brought with him. With jerky motions, he stuffed the pack with his belongings before going to the bathroom and doing the same.

He paused near the bed for a hard look at Diamond. Her position allowed him to see the contours between her legs. Though upset, he was aroused, but it was going to take more than that to hold him. "I can't believe I let you talk me into this snitch-ass shit, anyway!"

Diamond was suddenly off the bed and in his face. At 5'4," she was about seven inches shorter, having to look up to meet his gaze. "So, what? You're done with me too?" Her voice broke. Her eyes watered. "After all we've been through, you're leaving me to deal with this alone?"

He didn't want to leave her alone. He wanted to take her into his arms, strip off those revealing boy shorts and suck on the luscious mound between her legs. He wanted to make love and try to convince her that this was all insane. He would, however, succeed in all but the latter, and he'd wind up content in bed beside her thereafter.

"Fuck you!" Garrett shot back, refusing to give in. "You're worse than a bitch with no ass who don't suck dick. Useless!" With nothing more, he slung the pack over his shoulder and stormed out of the room.

Garrett's heated exchange with the guard outside the door was audible, but the actual words were lost to Diamond as she retreated, disheartened, and dejected, to the bed and into her private thoughts.

Useless! His words echoed in her mind. *Like a bitch with no ass who don't suck dick.*

Diamond was struck by Garrett's assessment. Although she was small, her ass was fat, and she did suck dick. More than that, she loved him, and he knew that as well. So why then was he giving her a hard time about the situation? Was he right about it all? Would it be best for her to follow his lead and stay in her own lane? Garret was well aware of her sentiment regarding the youth. With that, how could he expect her to remain idle and let the men in question get away with the ruthless act of murdering two innocent people?

She was crying silently now, confused, and with tears running down her pretty, yellow cheeks, she took up her cellphone and called the only person she could under the circumstances.

“Hello?” Nae answered energetically.

“We got into it again,” Diamond blurted. “This time, he broke up with me.”

“What for this time?”

“Same as before; he doesn’t want me to testify, and he wants nothing more to do with the situation.” Diamond nearly choked on a sob. “He walked out on me, Nae!”

Nae cared deeply for her younger sister. Although she would never testify in the manner Diamond was all set to do, she knew grief at the girl's distress. However, she supported her sister’s decision and would never make her feel as if she had no one to turn to. With that, she forced herself to say, “I think you’re doing the right thing. Just give Garrett a little space; he’ll come around. Besides, didn’t you say the trial was right around the corner?”

“Next month, the D.A said, if neither of them takes a plea.”

“In that case, I think it’s safe to say you’ll have Garrett’s head back between your legs in about a month.”

That made Diamond smile. “Um, what makes you think he’s doing all of that?”

“You sayin’ he isn’t?”

Diamond’s smile broadened. "I'm not."

“Like I thought,” Nae asserted. “Now, get some rest. This will all be over before you know it.”

“Thanks, Nae.”

“No problem,” Nae said. “Love you.”

"I love you too." Diamond broke the connection with a silent prayer for God to bring Garrett back into her life. As if that would be the case immediately, she checked her iPhone's message box, finding several, but neither were from the man she wanted. She caught sight of her reflection and the fact her Amber Rose haircut was in need of a shapeup. She sat her phone aside and considered the true event that lay ahead of her, the decision to testify at the trial.

At age four, two years younger than her sister Nae, Diamond found herself subjected to the perverted hands of their stepfather, Frank, who began with acts of oral sex he coaxed them to perform on him. By age ten, he was buying thongs for Diamond to wear as she performed the act. He was having intercourse with Nae at twelve. His preference, however, was for Diamond. By her twelfth birthday, Frank was breaking her in from the front and the back.

At some point, Diamond took to the experience and welcomed her stepfather's advances with open arms. She was servicing him without having to be questioned, commanded, or told. It was to the point where Diamond would pretend to be sick, staying home from school to share intimate moments with Frank. It was in this manner they were caught.

Diamond's mother, Marlene, a CNA at Winnwood Retirement Community, was hard at work but was concerned for her teen daughter sick at home. Having called several times with no answer, Marlene took off early with the mind to hurry home to see about her daughter. Frank's truck was in the driveway when it shouldn't have been. She opened the door to silence, but midways onto the staircase, the faint but unmistakable sounds of sexual exclamations became increasingly clear.

No good, sneaky bastard, was her initial thought.

But as she neared her own bedroom with its open door and neatly made bed, she knew a measure of relief that it wasn't Frank in violation. She actually felt a measure of guilt for her initial assumption. Frank had been nothing but a loving husband who had given exceptional care to her daughters.

Drawn further down the hall, it was clear that one of her teenage girls, having come into themselves, was currently indulging the act. Certain it was her oldest daughter, Nae, Marlene walked purposefully to the girls' room. Sex was natural, and she wasn't all that upset. However, she was going to make clear that she wouldn't tolerate the act under her roof.

Marlene threw open the door, prepared to reprimand Nae and the boy she was with. But Marlene choked at the sight that greeted her; it wasn't Nae whose knees were pinned near to her head, and it wasn't a boy who possessed her in that manner. It was her husband, Frank, with her fifteen-year-old daughter, Diamond, and the manner in which she accommodated his seemingly ferocious advance made clear this wasn't his first time with her.

Frank, startled at Marlene's sudden appearance, was quick to release the young girl, who ran naked and crying down the hall and into the bathroom.

Frank couldn't speak, let alone meet Marlene's gaze. Through his mask of shame, he was left scurrying for his clothes as she went, fueled by rage, downstairs and into the kitchen. With trembling hands, she picked up the phone and dialed 911.

Moments later, when Frank appeared with his sorry excuse, Marlene was opening the side door for two police officers. Frank took note and broke for the back door, but was stopped in his tracks by an electric charge from one of the officer's issued tasers. Nine months after his arrest, he went to trial thinking he would win the case for whatever reason and was sentenced to life in prison. Marlene was a wreck, thereafter, feeling as if she had failed Diamond as a mother and protector. For months, she'd cry just looking at Diamond. And when Nae had eventually told her that she'd been molested by Frank as well, it made matters worse.

Frank wrote to Marlene, proclaiming it wasn't him that was hurting the girls, but an evil spirit instead. Marlene never replied. She died of a heart attack a year after his trial, having stressed herself to death.

CHAPTER 2

This nigga got a boss out here playing hookup, Ken thought, turning his white Range Rover into the strip plaza. He was in the city of Atlanta, the community of Pittsburgh to be exact, and guided here by GPS. He parked in front of a salon, checking the market signs to ensure his current location was the correct one. A Family Dollar, an American Deli, and a Universal Salon & Supplies were present.

J-Bo had mentioned the fact that the girl worked at some hair salon on the south side, but he couldn't say where exactly. With that, Ken had searched Google for salons within the specified area. He'd gotten six addresses and phone numbers. He called each in turn. Five of them claimed to have no employee or member known as Nae.

"Please hold," was what he was told by one as they went in search of the girl. Ken didn't hold, of course. Instead, assuming he'd gotten his mark, he broke the connection and entered the location into his GPS.

Only for J-Bo, Ken thought as he got out of his vehicle. The two had been close friends for ten years in counting. Ken and Flip were cool, too, but J-Bo was his main man. They met at the age of sixteen while visiting J-Bo's school to watch the football game.

Ken's initial encounter with J-Bo was supposed to be nothing more than a simple exchange. Ken wanted some weed for the game and had peeped J-Bo trapping near the bathroom. With that, he approached with a minimum of words and a ten-dollar bill in hand. "Let me get one."

"Fa'sho." J-Bo glanced quickly about before accepting the money and putting it into his pocket. He passed Ken a sack of popcorn mid and, Ken went about his business.

He had barely gotten out of earshot when the commotion from J-Bo's spot caught his attention.

"You got me fucked up," J-Bo spat at three niggas hovering threateningly close. "I ain't givin' y'all shit!"

They were attempting to shake him down, but the lil nigga was bucking the jack. Ken was a fighter, and he loved to see others fight. With that, he retraced his steps to watch, recognizing the perpetrators as the ringleader step closer to J-Bo.

"You betta run dat sack before we beat yo ass and take it!"

J-Bo wasn't backing down. "Y'all pussy ass niggas can try, but-"

He didn't finish; the ringleader struck his face with a hard right, knocking him back and to one side. The others followed suit, raining down punches before J-Bo could recover. He was dropped by a particularly hard blow and was bombarded with even more punches and kicks. Between which, he was able to detect Ken's approach, certain the big dude was there to contribute to the beat down.

Ken threw a strong hook to the temple of one of J-Bo's attackers, dropping him immediately. His startled partna took a swing at Ken, who ducked quick and slid in behind the boy, snatching him up in a death choke and choking him until he passed out. Ken slung him to the ground.

With only one opponent to contend with, J-Bo was able to shine. He caught the ringleader's upraised foot with both hands and swept the boy's leg out from under him, bringing him down hard to the ground. J-Bo rolled and came quick to his feet. The ringleader was just as quick. Aware now of his disadvantage, he took a second look at his unconscious companions and took off running.

"Damn, shawty," J-Bo wiped his busted lip with his shirt as he left the scene at Ken's side, blending in with the crowd.

"I appreciate dat." He went in his pocket and gave Ken a free sack. Ken nodded. "I had an issue with them nigga's anyway." He pocketed the weed and made an attempt to break away.

"Wait." J-Bo hurried to catch up. "What's yo name?"

"My name is Ken." His irritation was clear. "Peep game. I'm not looking for friends. I had a lil beef with them already. That's the only reason I helped you." He walked away to enjoy the game and his high, but J-Bo followed, persistent with conversation Ken didn't want. In spite of Ken's initial assessment, he kept company with J-Bo, and they eventually became the best of friends.

****

Ken entered the salon to the smell of singed hair, chemicals, and shampoo, surreptitiously analyzing the women in search of Nae, a fine ass yellow bone according to J-Bo's description.

"Hello, sir?" the greeting was from a woman who matched the description. "Can I help you?"

"I'm looking for Nae," Ken said.

"I'm Nae. What can I do for you?"

She spoke as if she knew him already. Not only was she physically attractive, but her attitude was also nice.

He peered at the other working girls, then back to Nae. "I need my dreads re-twisted."

He really didn't want a stranger touching his hair, but that was the only pretense for his presence.

"I got you," she flashed her whites flirtatiously. "But first, how do you know my name?"

Ken smiled, caught off guard by the question. But he was quick on his feet. "A friend told me you were the best."

"Mr.," one of the working girls chimed in a flirtatious manner. "We're all the best."

Neither he nor Nae acknowledged the comment.

"That's what's up," Nae shot back. "I like ya outfit."

Ken sported a simple white tailored shirt that hugged his toned muscles, some white jeans looped by a Gucci belt, and a pair of low-top, white, green, and red Gucci shoes. "Thank you."

"Uh-huh. Follow me," Nae directed.

Ken followed, looking at her plump booty. They went well with her c-cup breast. He once had a girl that looked just like her. Nae's hair was longer, and he wondered about the facial expression she would make if he was fucking and pulling her hair at the same time. He wondered if it was natural.

Nae reached a chair towards the back, told Ken to have a seat, and he did just that. As she prepared all of her materials and equipment, she realized she hadn't quoted him yet. With that, she said, "That's gonna be $125, Mr. Long Hair Man."

With him relaxed in the recliner and with her standing over him, she glanced at the Rolex he sported on his left wrist and wondered if it was real.

"No problem, Beautiful," he flirted.

Nae smiled, and the girl who had spoken earlier sucked her teeth. Nae cut her eyes at the girl. "Reisha, girl, cut that shit out before you find yourself looking for another job."

The girl then said nothing, and Ken decided he liked Nae's aggression as well.

She pumped the foot lever to recline the seat, and at that moment, he started in on her.

"I noticed no ring on those delicate and nimble fingers of yours. A beauty like yourself, and no one's trying to tie you down."

"Um. What makes you think I'm not tied down, and I just don't wear my ring to work?"

Ken laughed, seriously liking everything about the girl. "There's not even a faint impression of a ring on the finger that matters. But that's not to say you don't have a boyfriend- or a girlfriend if you get down like that."

"Ooh," Nae said. "Aren't you something?" She sighed, met his gaze, and said, "No husband, no man or girlfriend, because I don't get down like that." She smiled teasingly, dipping her fingers into the Mango Lime Twists, and gripping his new growth. "What about you?"

Damn, he thought. *She even has a nice sense of humor.* "The same for me," he said, hoping she would take control of the conversation. He wasn't used to spitting game. With his rising success with music, women seem to flock to his side without so much as a word from him. He considered it all a matter of luck, and luck was with him today. Nae caught sight of YBE tatted between his eyes and asked him what it stood for.

"It's the initials of my record label."

"Oh, you rap?" She was put off by the idea. Every guy she met, it seemed, wanted to be a rapper. She rolled her eyes, no longer impressed.

"I don't rap." Ken was cocky with the fact. "I just own the label."

"Aaahh," Reisha said from across the room. "So, you own the label that Lil Dread is signed to?"

The mockery in her tone was clear, and if it wasn't clear there, it certainly was in everyone's laughter. Nae was the only one present who tried to conceal her amusement, wanting to spare Ken's feelings. Even so, it was just too damn funny. Lil Dread was a street rapper who was starting to elevate, transcending to rapping mainstream. There was no way the nigga in her chair was the owner of that label.

"I do," Ken broke into the group's laughter. "And Lil Dread is my artist and lil brother, smartass."

Ken caught sight of Reisha and noticed that she was the one who had made the slick comment about all of them being the best when he first entered. She was red-boned, skinny with a pixie cut hairstyle, and had a mouth like a horse. The kind of chick the guys would talk to because she was red, but if she was dark skin, they would swear she was ugly.

No wonder she's mad, Ken thought.

The salon was silent for the remainder of the time Nae spent on Ken's head. Reisha looked him over occasionally, checking out his designer clothes and his Rolex watch, wondering if he really is who he said he was.

Once Nae was finished and paid, Ken pulled out his iPhone X and went into his gallery. He actually didn't care whether they believe him or not, but he was here to get a job done, and he needed Nae.

"Let me show you something."

Nae looked at his screen, and all the others gathered around to see what he had to present. He showed them videos of himself with Lil Dread and other members together. There were photos of them in the studio, on the plane, and in various cities around the country. What set it off for them all is a video of Lil Dread acknowledging Ken as the big homie, without whom, his success wouldn't be possible.

Ken could see the looks on their face, see their calculating thoughts, and to set them all straight, he said. "I'm only interested in Nae."

Reisha was stuck on stupid. He'd noticed her sidelong glances after his initial claim, and he'd seen her open admiration when he presented the actual proof. He looked at each of them in turn, then said to Nae, "Come outside. Let's talk." He left without waiting for her reply.

"Ooh wee, girl. He's demanding," another girl said before Nae pocketed the bills and followed Ken outside.

He was leaning against a brand new 2018 Range Rover. Nae was impressed as she approached, all smiles to reflect that.

Although running game wasn't a strong point for Ken, he got straight to it with enough truth to get the job done; confident Nae had been bagged by his status.

"I came to your shop with only a name, looking for you to twist my dreads. Yeah, you fine, but it's your personality that's got me checking you out."

Nae folded her arms across her chest and shifted her weight to one foot. The gesture gave definition to her ass, jutting out to one side. "And?"

Ken chuckled. His smile was genuine. Nae's attitude was really something. "I want to get to know you." He glanced at his gold watch and said, "I got some business to handle. Give me your number so I can call you later." He pulled out his iPhone expectantly. Nae gave her number, and he locked it in.

"You smoke weed?" Ken asked.

"Only the best."

Nae offered a smile, different from any earlier displayed. "So, you wanna get to know me, like meet the family one day or?"

Ken was struck here as well. The girl was appealing even when shy and uncertain. He pulled her into a close embrace. "It may come to that." He had to tread carefully. "You have a big family?"

Nervous at first, she found his embrace soothing, restoring her usual confidence. "My mama passed away when I was a teenager, and my daddy is doing life in prison."

"Damn, boo. I'm sorry to hear that." He tightened his grip for a few seconds before releasing her.

"Yea, it's okay. But I have a lil sister. She's hella chill. You'll like her."

Now we're getting somewhere, Ken thought. "That's what's up, Love." He looked at his watch again. "But listen, I have a meeting that I can't afford to miss. I'll get at you later." He hopped in the Range and hauled ass.

****

"Jerome and Phillip Dew!" An officer called from the dorm's entrance. He was reading from a clipboard. "Attorney visit!" J-Bo and Flip, seated at the spades table, threw down their cards at hearing their names. They walked out the dorm entrance, and the officer escorted them to a small room down the hall with only a picnic table and a few plastic lawn chairs. A short, rounded man stood to meet them.

"Hi, fellas." It was their attorney, John Luis. He was around forty years of age. He shook their hands. "How are you guys?"

"Hopefully better after this visit" J-Bo spoke for the both of them. They took their seats, and the escort officer took up his position near the door. He was present at all times for the attorney's sake.

"Can I have some privacy with my clients, please?" Mr. Luis asked the officer.

"Are you sure you want to be in here alone with them, sir?"

Mr. Luis laughed. "I'm sure. Thank you."

The officer nodded and left. Mr. Luis' fake smile vanished, and he scoffed as soon as the door closed. He was a Jew. His skin was pale, and he was going bald up top. He didn't give a damn. His money was long enough to buy whatever hair restoration procedure he wanted. He sat down, took a deep breath, and released a heavy sigh, running his hand down his face before unbuttoning his jacket. He leaned forward in his seat and whispered, "That damn witness is the only thing making my job hard."

The escort officer was staring hard through the window. Luis locked eyes with him, and the man turned his back completely, giving them the privacy that he'd requested. "The DA is tired of fucking around. He's offering you both a split sentence of forty do thirty, first and final offer."

"And when we say motha-fuck no?" J-Bo retorted.

Mr. Luis sat back, throwing his hands up. "Trial begins in a month or so."

"Mr. Luis, I gave you $75,000. That's way too much money for a high-ass plea like dat," J-Bo snapped. "We ain't takin' no fuckin-"

"Yes," Mr. Luis acceded, cutting J-Bo off, replicating the man's heated tone. "Way too much money, but not too much for a high-profile case where two teens and a fucking unborn child were murdered. No less with a fucking eyewitness calling the police from the crime scene, describing in detail the very events you are denying." He pointed to Flip. "Cap that off with the license plate given matching that of a truck registered to you." He paused. "Let me put it to you this way. She comes to court, and you're toast."

A heavy silence filled the room. The implication was clear. Though he'd paid the man handsomely, attorneys weren't all set against treachery. J-Bo wasn't about to divulge the fact that they were in the process of knocking the opponent's queen off the board.

J-Bo shot Flip a quick glance, and they rose simultaneously from their seats. “We’ll see how it all plays out,” J-Bo said. “But we ain’t taking them pleas. He got us fucked up.”

CHAPTER 3
THREE WEEKS LATER

"How my butt look in these?" Diamond asked, twirling to show off the new booty shorts she ordered from an up-and-coming designer.

Nae squeezed Diamond's ass. "Juicy."

Diamond laughed, swatted Nae's hand, and took a seat beside her on the couch. "Anyway, what about this nigga you were talking about?"

Nae smiled.

"Damn, you smiling like that. You sure he ain't stuck no dick in you yet?"

Nae sucked her teeth. "His name is Ken, and no, he hasn't stuck no dick in me yet." There was a noticeable emphasis on the last word. "I just met him the other week, bitch. I'm not a thot like you."

Diamond rolled her eyes. "Where he work at, girl?"

"He owns that rap label. YoungBoss," she said proudly.

Diamond's smile became a frown. "I know you ain't talking about YoungBoss, where that sexy ass nigga Lil Dread be shouting out in all his songs." She laughed.

"Well, to correct you, that's my boo's label, and he pays Lil Dread's lil broke ass."

"Girl, how the hell did you meet him?"

"He came in the salon, and I hooked his dreads up. Oh yea, girl, I had to chump Reisha's ugly ass off, too." Nae was in the middle of relaying the events that transpired on the day she met Ken when she was silenced by a knock on the door. It opened before either of them could reply.

A security team member stuck his head in. "Ms. Waters, I'm leaving. The other shift has arrived. Do you need anything?"

Diamond shook her head, no, and he closed the door.

"Uh girl," Nae complained. "That was rude. We could've been in here talking about anything and his ugly, American Dad looking-ass gone just open the door."

"They'll learn one day, girl. The other one opened the door, one day while I was trying to suck the skin off Garrett's dick, talking bout do I need anything."

Nae busted out laughing. "What you tell him, girl?"

She smiled innocently. "Didn't mama tell us not to talk with a mouthful?"

"You are so fucking nasty!" she exclaimed, knowing damn well she was too, just not as flamboyant. She was laughing so hard her stomach hurt.

"But back to Ken, though. I wish I could've met him first." She poked her lip out.

"Whatever, girl, but I told him about mama, daddy, and you."

"What about me?" She rubbed her nipples.

"Diamond, you are a slut!" she laughed.

"Duhh!"

Nae's phone went off, bringing a smile to her face as she looked at the screen. She put her finger to her lips for silence and answered, "Hey boo. Uh no, I'm not. Yea, that's fine. Okay, give me half an hour." She listened for a few more seconds before hanging up.

"That was him, girl." Nae pulled Diamond up for a hug before snatching her purse from the couch. "He wants me to meet him at Maggiano's in Buckhead," she quickly explained, rushing for the door.

Nae had heard of the place plenty of times, but she had never made it her business to check it.

I guess today will be the day, she thought.

"Love you, bitch!" Diamond called after her. "Be careful!"

"Love you, too!"

****

Ken turned into the parking lot and spotted Nae standing on the curb looking gorgeous. He parked and removed the .45 from the passenger seat and slid it under his seat. He reached in the glove compartment and pulled a bottle of YSL sports cologne out, spraying the collar of his white Gucci dress shirt.

After leaving Diamond's room, Nae had gone to the nearest Kohl's to purchase a black and white sundress. It complimented her petite frame and was a perfect match for her white earrings and black slides.

"You look great." He hugged her. Her lemon midrange skin appeared flawless, and she smelled edible.

She blushed. "Thank you, handsome."

Ken took her hand, and they walked towards the entrance to where he held the door open for her.

"Table for two," he told the beautiful Italian hostess at her station.

She offered a dazzling smile and presented menus for them both. "Right this way."

The place was elegant, filled with a caste group of people. Beneath their feet was thick, noticeably soft, white carpet. Above, expensive chandeliers were hung throughout, from where came a strategically dim light. A jazz melody was set accordingly, and those there to listen were mostly Italian. Small Italy was the restaurant's nickname, and everyone there was dressed to impress.

Ken ordered shrimp pasta, Nae order lasagna, and they both had a taste for red wine. Sipping which, Nae asked, "Do you have kids?"

"No," came Ken's measured reply. "But I'm sure we can make some pretty babies."

"You are crazy." She smiled, cheeks turning red. "You go from dinner to babies."

He smiled teasingly. "I believe the tone was set by you."

"A bit altered by you. Besides, we don't know each other that well, so we probably shouldn't even be having this conversation."

Ken sat back, contemplating killing Nae's sister and maybe her as well. He stared into her mesmerizing eyes, gazed at her perfect white teeth and delicate full lips, aware of how beautiful she truly was.

"Real talk. Isn't this in preparation for us getting to know each other?"

"Here you are." The waitress was just as beautiful as the hostess. She sat their plates on the table before them. "Anything else?"

Ken shook his head. "No, thank you."

"Enjoy." She started to turn, then turned back. "You two are a very beautiful couple," she said before going about her business.

Nae was smiling ear to ear. "Did you pay her to say that?"

Ken swallowed a forkful of pasta. "Hell, If I hadn't made the arrangements here, I'd be asking you the same thing."

They shared a genuine laugh, and Ken was acutely aware that he hadn't been this way with a woman since high school. What he felt now were sensations he'd thought were dead forever.

"Ken," Nae spoke cautiously. "I'm not a groupie. It wouldn't matter to me if you were flipping burgers at McDonald's." She took a forkful of the cheesy lasagna.

He cocked an inquisitive brow, confused.

"I know it's early, but I like you, and I want you to treat me with respect."

Ken knew where she was coming from with that, and he responded accordingly. "I like you too, Nae." But the words weren't a game. He did like her, and he was increasingly aware of the dilemma. His mission was to kill her sister, but there was no denying his attraction to Nae. It's been so long since anyone has made him feel this way, and he wanted to see how far it could go. He thought of J-Bo and knew he had to pull it together. *I got you, lil bra.*

"Plus," Ken went on. "If I thought you were a groupie, we wouldn't even be here." He washed his food down with a sip. "We'd be at McDonald's."

Nae almost choked, suppressing a laugh while drinking from her glass. "You're so silly, Ken."

"So, do you own or lease the salon?"

"Ummm," she was uneasy discussing her personal finances with him. "I kinda own it, barring the fact I still owe the bank about fifteen grand. But I'll have that taken care of by the end of the year."

"Why wait so long for something you want now?"

Nae chuckled. "Now, isn't what I can afford."

"I can."

Nae sat her fork down and gave Ken her undivided attention. "What are you saying?"

"I'm saying the salon will be all yours tomorrow."

Nae stared. The implication was clear. "You can't be serious?"

"I can, and I am."

Nae was silent. Her mind raced. Her heart accelerated. Who was he to make such an offer? He said he liked her, but this was something beyond that. He wasn't offering fifteen-grand for a piece of ass. He could get elsewhere for less. And not to take anything from herself in the looks department, he could find better as well. She was no prostitute, but put in perspective, who could refuse?

"I-I don't understand." Nae had trouble finding her words. "What's going on here?"

Ken narrowed the distance between them, staring into her light brown eyes. "What I'm beginning to feel, I haven't felt in years. Read between the lines and *see* what's going on."

Her lips trembled, and for a second, she couldn't breathe. Was he really saying…

Her thoughts were lost as Ken leaned in, closing the remaining distance, and touched his lips to hers. Instinctively, she opened her mouth to his passionate kiss.

He broke away with a reluctant sigh, and they fell silent for several seconds thereafter, contemplating all said and implied. Though Nae liked Ken, she understood what it meant for him to make such an offer. So, too, what it meant for her to accept. Was she willing to go that far?

Ken, however, found himself face to face with the reason niggas catered to the girl they cared for. He was never with that; an offer from him, on the rare occasion, was a simple proposition. It wasn't the case here, and neither could he say the gesture was all a part of getting where he needed to be with her in order to get the job done.

CHAPTER 4

The next day the exact thing Nae had been hoping didn't occur, happened. She was at her workstation, busy with a client's hair, when he barged into the salon. The women looked up, smelling trouble as he passed. The stylists shared knowing glances with each other across the room, knowing well it was about to go down. Reisha was chewing bubblegum and smiling mischievously.

Nae, her back to the entrance, noticed the abnormal silence, turned- and gasped at the man who was now standing directly behind her.

Slick Nick was tall, red, and slim. With his low haircut and his animated personality, he reminded everyone of Mike Epps.

What the fuck are you doing here? Nae wanted to ask, but she knew already. They had been seeing each other for the past eight months, but with his insecure behavior regarding the smallest thing, Nae had decided to leave him. Ken's appearance and interest had been the icing on the cake. She and Slick Nick were history. The problem, however, is she had never given him closure.

"What's goin' on, shawty?" Slick Nick's tone was aggressive. "You been dodgin' a nigga fa weeks now. I mean, I am yo nigga, right?"

"Nick, can't you see I'm busy? We'll talk later." Nae rolled her eyes and turned back to her client's hair.

"No, the fuck we ain't." Slick Nick grabbed her shoulder and spun her around. "We gon' talk right fuckin' now!"

The outburst gained everyone's attention who wasn't looking already.

Damn, Reisha thought. You could hear a mouse piss on cotton. *Get that hoe, Nick!* Reisha didn't like Nae from the moment she was hired. She simply played it cool for the sake of keeping a job.

Nae was terribly embarrassed and didn't appreciate his behavior. "What the fuck, Nicholas? Don't you see I'm working?" She pointed to Tisha's half-done individuals. "You come by my fucking job making a big ass scene and shit. Got everybody and their fucking mamas in our business! I said we'll talk later."

"I don't care 'bout these hoes-" he gestured around the room as he spoke "-their hair or their fuckin' mamas. I wanna know why you been iggin' me!"

Nae couldn't believe he was actually pulling up this way. She considered not telling him about Ken, but decided it was something he should know. *Maybe he would get the fuck on then.*

"Fine," Nae relented. "Let's go outside." She wiped her hands with a towel. "Tisha, I'll be back in a minute." She turned to leave and was blocked by Nick's raised forearm. She frowned at the arm holding her back. "Nigga, what's your problem? I said we'd talk outside."

Nick's demeanor was calm all of a sudden.

There was hurt in his eyes and a glimmer of something else. She knew he had gotten the message. He just needed to hear it from the horse's mouth. "You shouldn't do things you'll regret."

"What the hell is that supposed to mean, Nicholas?"

"Whatever you gotta say outside, you can say in here."

"Nick, I don't wanna talk in front of eve-"

"Bitch, tell me what the fuck is goin' on!" he snapped. "You fuckin' wit anotha nigga or somethin'?" He took a step closer to her.

She felt guilty for not telling him earlier, and for not being grown about it before it came to this. Her heart was pounding, and her nerves were bouncing everywhere. "Yes, Nick. I'm seeing someone else, and it's over between us."

Nick rubbed his naked chin. "Over between you and that nigga, right? Or is it a bitch you fuckin' with?"

She saw cold fury in his eyes. At the same time, she didn't miss the escape route provided, one she was tempted to take. However, she was fed up with all the drama dealing with Nick. More than that, she was truly interested in what she had going with Ken.

Nae took a deep breath. "It's not a bitch, and it's over between you and me."

Nick's eyes narrowed to a slit. "So, you just gon' leave me that easy, shawty?"

****

Ken sat at the dining room table of his main spot on the west side, watching his brothers do what they do best. Some were weighing dope to go make plays, while others were in the near furniture-less living room shooting dice. Two younger brothers, comfortable on the long sectional, were watching "Baby Boy" on a 53-inch screen. Out of sight and in other rooms throughout the house, brothers were intimately involved with local thots.

The lights were dimmer in the living room than they were in the dining room, where Ken sat with Chingy. He approved the way his brother kept the trap house: no broken windows, no holes nor writing on the walls, and the furniture was intact with neither cuts nor burns to the upholstery. Most of all, the money was flowing expeditiously. Ken knew he'd appointed the right man for the job.

"So, that's two-hundred?" Ken asked, pointing to the blue duffle bag on the floor.

Chingy nodded. "Yea." He removed a small brown bag from a jacket pocket hanging on the back of his chair, emptying the sprucely stacked money on the table. "Here's thirty more right here, and I'll have the otha twenty in a minute."

Ken smiled, breaking the rubber band and feeding the bills to the small money counter on the table. "I swear you make me proud, Chingy."

"I just do what I'm supposed to, big bro. You feel me?" Chingy was a skinny dude. At twenty-one years old, he stood 5' 10" and weighed 150 pounds. He was the same complexion as Ken, and he thought it was still cool to wear cornrows in 2018. He was scratching an itch between one of his rows when his phone went off.

"Hello?" he answered. "Yea, I'm at the spot, shawty." He listened, then burst out laughing. "Ok, bro, just bring me sixty. I got you three of them thangs." He hung up. "That was my potna's lil brotha. He talking bout he gon' come get that pack this time because his brotha out tryna stalk his bitch." He almost choked on his laughter.

Chingy got up and removed three bricks from behind the refrigerator and laid them on the table.

Ken frowned, caressing his forehead. "Chingy, how the hell are you selling them for twenty a pop when I'm giving them to you like that? You can't make one cent that way."

Chingy laughed. "You talkin' bout this?" He pointed to the product. "It's mostly cut. I turn one into three."

There was a bottle of Patron on the table, from which Ken poured a shot and took it to the head. This was no game he'd given Chingy, and when questioned further, Chingy revealed that his cousin from Savannah had schooled him on how to cut and recompress.

Ken shook his head in dismay. “Young brother, you can’t do everybody like that. Shit like this will make us lose customers, as well as bring unnecessary problems with people.”

“Your work is pure enough to handle the cut. Niggas sellin’ cheap, so the clientele don’t complain.”

Ken took another shot of patron, and Chingy took one as well.

****

Nae had no chance to answer. Slick Nick followed his question with a punch square in the face, almost knocking her to the floor. She caught herself by latching on to Tisha’s chair, doubling over with a hand to her face. She cried out and spat a mouth full of warm blood.

“Bitch, I done invested way too much time and money for you to just up and leave me like dis!” His tears fell freely as he rained punches down on her.

The girls were terrified, frozen, and didn’t know what to do. Nae was trying, unsuccessfully, to block the onslaught of blows from her furious ex-lover.

“This my pussy!” Nick screamed. “You my bitch!” He dropped her with a particularly hard right. She balled up, and he started in on her with vicious kicks to her head and torso.

“Please!” Nae cried pitifully. “Somebody call 911.” She was silenced by a kick to the head. She was motionless as well, but Nick didn’t stop.

Tisha was the first to act, but not to call 911.

She jumped from her seat, looking for something to use as a weapon. Beside her chair were two hot curling irons that Nae had been using to straighten her hair. One of which she grabbed and rushed Nick, shouting, “Leave her alone, you bitch-ass nigga!” as she struck him across the back of the neck. Nick gave a cry of his own, and his next kick faltered and was of no consequence. He turned two furious eyes on his attacker, pissed by her assault. He swung, catching her jaw in much the same way he'd caught Nae. But Tisha was a chunky woman, and she didn't budge.

"You ain't a man!" she spat through a pair of bloody lips. "You a pussy!" She swung the curling iron again, striking him over the left eye. He screamed, louder this time, having been struck in a spot more receptive to pain. He staggered back, pulled a .380 from his back pocket. The terrified women weren't frozen anymore. They were all up and about, screaming, ducking, hiding behind chairs, and running out of the shop to safety. Tisha stood her ground and was brutally struck across the face with Nick's automatic. Though she was chunky, the blow sent her crashing to the floor, where she remained, unconscious. Nick looked at the motionless women and fled the scene.

****

In a plastic chair, at the plastic table in the trap house's dining room, Ken studied the $20,000 watch on his wrist. He wanted an upgrade. But he couldn't do so until Lil Dread's touring gained momentum. A careless purchase now would bring the feds on his ass. However, his primary attention to the watch was in regard to time. He had made several attempts to call Nae, and he had gotten no answer. It was getting late; she should have returned his call by now. More to that, he'd be in the trap house for the rest of the night. It was all part of his quarterly routine checkup where he'd stay the entire day to monitor all the trap's arrangements and activities.

"Somebody get the door, shawty." Chingy called out to those in the living room. He knew who was there; Mario had just sent him a text saying he was outside.

A brown skin dread-head YoungBoss affiliate opened the door, and the first thing he noticed was the tightly wrapped Kroger bag in Mario's hand. He eyed it suspiciously.

"It's just some money, shawty."

The YoungBoss affiliate looked him over, allowed him to enter, then led him to the dining room with Chingy, who was seated at the plastic dining room table with Ken, counting money. On top of the table were the bricks that Mario had come to purchase. Chingy stood to greet him, embracing him with a handshake hug before both of them took their seat at the table.

Chingy could barely contain his laughter. "So, what da hell dis nigga got goin' on, shawty?"

"Man, this nigga talkin' bout he gotta holla at his hoe real quick. I'm like nigga we got business to handle. That shit can wait. He talkin' bout the hoe won't come to da doe, so he finna break in the hoe house. I'm like, maaan. I just left his ass. Whoever the bitch is, she got bra fucked up. No flex." Mario dropped the Kroger's bag on the table

Ken ripped through the bag and began feeding the money to the machine.

Chingy decided to entertain the dumb shit. "That nigga hell. So, he was breaking in da hoe's house?"

Mario nodded, pulling a knife from his pocket. He cut into one of the packages on top of the table and tested it. He held the back of his hand to his nose and sniffed hard. A tear fell from his eye, and he wiped it away. "That's good coke." He placed the bricks in the Kroger bag and retied where Ken had ripped. Mario dapped both of them up and went on his way. The YoungBoss followed close behind.

Chingy took the money from the counter, fed it little by little to the money machine until it read $20,000. He handed it to Ken, held up the other forty, and laughed. “I just made an easy forty from two thousand grams of bullshit.”

Ken added the $20k to the small duffle bag on the floor.

“What’s good wit’ J-Bo and Flip. They still fightin’ dem bodies?”

Ken nodded, zipping the bag. “I got something in motion, though.”

“You need some help?”

“Nah, homie. It’s just a little female in the way. When the time is right, I’ll clap her.”

“Let me handle it.” Chingy insisted.

“Nah, but I’ll ring your line if I need you.”

Chingy got up and went to the kitchen, where he opened the cabinet and pulled out a black tech-nine “Yea, do dat homie, cuz I got a new bitch. Her name is Takia.” He held it up, admiring the breathing holes on the end of the barrel and the sixty-round extension attached. “She don’t get hot. She don’t jam. She just fuck.”

Ken stood, taking in the weapon. “Is that right? He took the gun from his young protégé.

****

“Ma’am, do you know where you are?” Someone asked, shining a bright light in Nae's eyes.

She squinted, using her hand to block the brightness. “No,” she answered groggily.

“Do you know your name?” The man asked, shutting the light off.

“Yes, I’m Nae Waters.” Her eyes adjusted to the room, and she knew she was in a hospital.

“Good,” he said. The coat labeled him the doctor. He was slim, black, and baldheaded. “You were picked up from a hair salon. The only reason you're here at Grady is because the other hospital's head trauma unit isn't as up to date as ours. But it's not what they thought because you're awake. It was a regular concussion. I'll release you in a day or two." He pointed to the red call button attached to the bed. "Press the button if you need me."

He left, and Nae glanced around the dimly lit room. She recognized a familiar frame seated on the sofa.

"Tisha?" she called out.

"Yea, girl, it's me." She went to Nae's bedside. Her head was wrapped with gauze and tape, and treated cuts were on her lips.

"Girl, what happened?"

Tisha shook her head. "You were unconscious, and he still wouldn't stop. I hit him with the hot iron, and he hit me with his iron."

"Aww, Tish, I'm so sorry. I appreciate it, but you know you didn't have to." A few tears rolled down her bloated cheeks.

Tisha waved her off. "Girl, please. I couldn't sit there like them other hoes did. Oh yea, I thank I saw ya girl crack a smile. The ugly one with no booty."

"Oh, Reisha? Yea, she's a hater. She's also fired."

That made Tisha smile.

"How long have I been here?" Nae didn't know if it was night or day.

Tisha looked at her phone. "Twelve hours."

"Did they bring my phone?" she looked around.

Tisha pointed to where the phone sat, charging on a mobile table. "Ken kept calling, and then it went dead, so I put it on my charger."

"Thank you, girl. Do you need a job?"

Tisha sucked her teeth. "Girl, I can't do hair."

"I'll teach you."

"Anyway." Tisha rolled her eyes and pointed to her half-done head. "I need to get this shit done."

"Hand me my phone." Nae held out her hand. "I'll call Reisha and make her finish it for free before I fire her."

CHAPTER 5

"I was on da grind... I was on da grind... I was on da grind, yea dat was my nine to five," J-Bo sang aloud, leaving the shower, on the way to his cell. The song, *On The Grind,* was a popular track by his homie, Lil Dread.

Flip was on his bunk sleep when J-Bo entered. He was putting on deodorant when he noticed there was only one Coca-Cola on the table; two were there before he'd gone to the shower. They were supposed to make a Bombay, but J-Bo figured his cousin had decided against that and may have drunk the soda instead. But then he recalled that Flip had been asleep before he'd gone to the shower.

Done with the application of lotion and baby powder, J-Bo stood and slapped Flip's foot. "Aye say, foo!"

Flip sat up, wiping his eyes. "Shiiid, I was tryna sleep. Wassup?"

"You moved that soda?" J-Bo threw a thumb gesture over his shoulder.

"What?" Flip looked at the table. "Hell, naw. These niggas trippin'."

J-Bo's eyes narrowed. "Make an announcement."

"Say no moe."

Flip put on his shoes and went to make the announcement while J-Bo got fully dressed and put on his own shoes. He wasn't hurting for commissary; they both had nearly $10,000 on their books. This was a matter of principle. J-Bo was furious to have any nigga take anything from him.

> "Aye, man," Flip yelled from the top range to the sixty-man dorm. "Who came in my room and took da soda off da table?"

No one responded. Everyone kept about minding their business.

J-Bo removed another soda from his property box and called out to Flip, "Put a numba on em."

"I got a hunnet dollas for whoeva tell me who took my shit!"

That got everybody's attention and all movement stopped. Everyone's eyes were glued to Flip.

J-Bo stood in the doorway. He was mixing coffee, Kool-Aid, and a little of the Coke all together in a bowl. "Go, higher, cuz."

"I got two-hunnet dollas on ya books right now! Fa whoeva tell me who came in my room and got my shit!"

This got their attention. A $200 store call in most jails was "rich nigga" status.

"Quan took it!" Fish blurted out from the spades table. He was 17 years old and was down for armed robbery. During his eight months of incarceration, he'd gone to the store once, and that was with the money he had in his pockets upon his arrest. With nothing coming in from family nor friends, the offer was too much to pass up.

"Fish," Quan barked from his room. "You a bitch-ass nigga! I'ma beat yo pussy ass!" He was about to run up on Fish, but the two cousins met him at his door before he could cross the threshold.

"Why you take it?" J-Bo asked.

"I-I was thirsty, shawty. Ain't think y'all would notice." His hands were shaking.

Quan was down for three counts of theft and two counts of armed robbery. He still hadn't learned his lesson about stealing.

Flip shouldered around J-Bo and leaped towards Quan, striking him over the eye with his balled fist.

"Bitch-ass-nigga," J-Bo growled, following through with blows of his own. The dorm looked on in silence, with an occasional "Ohhh or owe!" to emphasize particularly hard licks.

Quan's nose and mouth were leaking when the cousins were done with him.

"Get on da doe!" J-Bo commanded.

Discombobulated, leaking, and stumbling, Quan fled the cell and ran for the entrance door, pressing the emergency call button. He was near to panic with his press, looking back as if he expected J-Bo and Flip to appear and administer a second beating. The door opened, and Quan nearly knocked the floor officer down in his haste to get out.

"Fish!" J-Bo called out, dragging all of Quan's property to the door. "Grab da mop!"

J-Bo and Flip had blood on their hands, and J-Bo's shirt was splotched as well. They cleared all traces of the incident, and Fish was there in J-Bo's cell and in the process of giving them his deposit information when an officer stuck his head in the dorm and called, "Dew?"

Pen and paper in hand, J-Bo paused, exchanging quizzical glances with Flip and Fish.

"Which one?" someone asked.

"Jerome!" The officer replied.

"Quan's bitch-ass prolly snitched on me," J-Bo said. He looked at Fish, then turned to Flip. "If I go to da hole, make sure shawty get his money."

Flip nodded.

****

Quan didn't snitch; J-Bo had a visitor there to see him. However, the officer didn't miss the opportunity to question the matter.

"Jerome," the escorting officer said. "Who did that to that boy in the dorm? I swear to God, they won't know you told me." The officer clearly thought he had a duck.

"Nigga, you got me fucked up," J-Bo snapped.

****

Shakeena was there in the visitation room. Fine, chocolate, and thick like Nicki, she'd been his girl all through high school, and he'd been all set to marry the girl. But the night of his arrest put an end to that plan. He called her line several times and got no answer. He had Ken three-way her once, and the line went dead the moment she heard his voice. Subsequent calls were sent straight to voicemail thereafter. He'd heard nothing since. But here she was now, with an infant snuggled against her breast.

J-Bo glared at Shakeena, tempted to leave, but wanting answers, nevertheless. With that, he took a seat across from her and spoke through clenched teeth. "Man, shawty, what da fuck took you so long to come see me?"

"Baby, I'm soooo sorry. I was so depressed when they took you away from me. Then when I saw your charges, I- I just didn't know how to handle it." She cried a little before regaining control of herself. "When I found out I was pregnant, I had a nervous breakdown. And with everybody in my ear, telling me how bad it was and what they were going to do to you, I just couldn't face you." She hoped he would understand.

J-Bo nodded at the bundle in her arms. "How old is he?"

She smiled down at the baby. "Two months."

J-Bo glanced at the ceiling, counting the months on his fingers.

"Nigga!" Shakeena was pissed. "I found out I was pregnant a few days after you left me!" she snapped, and her tone made the baby fidget. "That was eleven months ago." She did the math for him. "It took me nine to have him."

J-Bo's expression was blank. "What's his name?"

"Jerome Dew, Jr." She smiled proudly, touching the baby's cheek. "But I like to call him JJ." She paused, then bombarded him with a series of questions. "So, what's up with your case? What are they saying? How is Flip doing? Do you get to see him?"

"I wrote you bout fifty letters, Shakeena."

"I know." She fought back threatening tears. "And I'm really sorry, Jerome. I was going through so much at the time. But I'm here now, and I swear to God none of it will ever happen again."

J-Bo's anger was hot. He hadn't realized to what degree until now. There was nothing she could say or do to make things peaches and cream.

"I put money on the phone if you decide to call me, Jerome." The baby started to wake, making soft noises. "Hey, JJ," she cooed as he stretched and yawned. "Hey, mama's baby boy." He opened his little round eyes. "You wanna go to daddy?" She tried to hand J-Bo the baby, but he didn't budge, let alone move to receive him.

Shakeena, the baby in her outstretched arms, frowned. "Jerome?"

J-Bo stood up and motioned for an officer. "Aye, man!" he called out to whoever cared to escort him back to the dorm. "I'm done."

"Jerome quit acting like that! This is your son!"

"Go to child support, and they'll come swab me."

****

The morning rays were shining through the white, and Nae was alone watching the *Wendy Williams Show* when an older Caucasian man was at her hospital bed, introducing himself as Detective Walker. He was slim, and his brown hair had begun to fade gray. Looking at the man, Nae couldn't shake the impression he was a dirty cop.

"I'm here to ask you a few questions about your attack yesterday," Detective Walker said.

Nae didn't like talking to the police. It usually followed with testifying in court. The idea brought to mind her sister's cooperation with the D.A. The difference here, however, was the fact Nae had been attacked and was a victim while her sister was sticking her nose in other people's business, snitching.

Walker asked a million questions about the incident. Time, date, location, the reason behind Nick's attack, his full name, phone number, and address. He jotted everything down on a small notepad. He thanked her and said he would be in touch.

Walker turned to leave but paused. "By the way," he said, "I'll be sure to kick his ass for you when I catch up to him."

Nae laughed. Her body ached when she did, and she winced. "Shoot his ass, too."

"Hopefully, he reaches for his cellphone," Walker said, passing a clipboard carrying Dr. Rasool on his way out.

"Ms. Waters, I see you're up early this morning. How are you feeling?"

"I'm fine, Doc." She smiled.

"Your tests are in. You're all good. I'll clear your release today."

"Thanks, Doc."

"Also," He looked at the clipboard in hand. "You have a visitor by the name of K. Griffith. He's not the guy, is he? The one that did this to you. If so, I can have the detective get him now."

"That won't be necessary." She was smiling from ear to ear. "He's my boo," she said proudly.

Dr. Rasool nodded and left the room. Ken entered with a dozen roses. He took in her appearance, and the roses were abandoned at the table as he rushed to her bedside, speechless by her appearance and by what he felt as a result. For several seconds he stared. Then he took her hand.

"Nae, tell me no one put their hands on you."

Her voice was soft when she spoke. "I wish I could tell you otherwise, but my ex beat me up when I told him about you."

He closed his eyes for a moment. "What's his name?"

"I already gave the detective his info, baby. Don't worry about it."

He sensed that she thought she was sparing him from having to play tough guy, but she had no idea of what he was capable of.

"Nae, baby, let's get something straight. When I ask a question, I want honest and accurate answers. Understand me?"

Her understanding was clear. "His name is Nick."

"He play in the streets?"

She nodded.

"He sells dope?"

She nodded again. "His ugly-ass brother, Mario, called me this morning, talking about he will pay me $2,500 not to tell the police. I hung straight up on him."

Ken took a seat in one of the cushion chairs, contemplating what Nae had told him. There was only one Nick he knew of that was trapping. The man was married and sported his wife everywhere. He had two sisters and no brothers, so it couldn't be him.

"Just, Nick?" Ken asked, "Or something else?"

"Slick Nick," Nae replied. "You think you know him or something?" She was concerned. "Baby, why does it matter?"

"Nae, stop questioning me." He got up and kissed her forehead. "I can't see you like this. Call me when they release you."

She sat up and called after him, but he walked out. She released a heavy sigh and laid back just as her phone started to ring.

"Hello?" she answered

"Girl, I've been calling yo ass since yesterday!" Diamond's voice blared through the receiver. "Angela told me what happened, and, of course, these fucking guards won't let me leave, ugh. Are you okay?"

"Yea, baby, I'm good. It was Nick's punk-ass, mad because I don't want his insecure ass no more." She felt sick just mentioning his name.

"Ooh-wee," Diamond stressed. "I hope somebody kills that bitch-ass-nigga!"

"Don't talk like that, Diamond."

"Nae, after this trial, I want to move... just the two of us. Fuck this inner-city shit. Let's get us a spot in Cobb or Gwinnett. You can even move the shop there. I just want to be away from all this crazy-ass shit."

Nae smiled, imagining her and her sister in a nice suburban area, living a normal and peaceful life, something they've never done before. "Diamond, I'm exhausted. I need a nap. We'll start looking for places soon. I'll call you. I love you, baby."

****

Ken was speeding on the expressway heading to Chingy's spot. Still, he wasn't certain why he felt slighted by Nae's attack. True, she was only a mission, a means to an end. Yet, she wasn't the target. With that, couldn't he like and care for her a little as long as he got the job done when it was time to do so? Yes, he reasoned. But on the flip side, he felt like a simp, paying off her loan, on the lookout for her attacker- and he hadn't even gotten the pussy yet. But pussy was applesauce to a boss, that which he could have at any given moment. At the end of the day, she was going to turn it in.

However, this Slick Nick guy needed to be dealt with. With that foremost in mind, he dialed Chingy's number.

"Yo?" Chingy answered.

"Slick Nick," Ken said. "You know the name?" The line was quiet. Ken looked at the phone, checking the connection. "Hello?"

"Yea, my bad fam, I fuck with shawty. How you know him?"

"I'll explain in person. But you fuck with him on what level?"

"I serve him. You remember Lil Mario that came to the spot last night?"

Mario, Ken thought. Where else had he heard the name?

"His ugly-ass brother, Mario, called me this morning," Nae's words came back to him. *"Talking about he will pay me $2,500 to not tell the police. I hung straight up on him."*

Ken put the pieces together. "That's his brother, right?"

"Yea. How da hell you know these folks, big bruh?"

"Slick Nick has violated me in a major way. I need him slammed ASAP." Having called the shot, he broke the connection.

****

Ken's office was located in downtown Atlanta. He sat behind his big glass desk, looking over paperwork and monitoring the few cameras he had installed around the small building. He liked to know that people were doing exactly what he paid them to do. His office was the largest in the one-story building, furnished with Louis V. chairs, rugs, carpet, and sofas. The suits in his closet were Louis V. He even had a few bottles of Louis V. in the refrigerator.

In pursuing the mission for J-Bo and Flip, Ken had fallen behind in his duties as a C.E.O, and he'd decided to come in and catch up. The truth, however, is that Ken couldn't get Nae and that clown ass nigga Slick Nick off his mind. The thought of her hurt and beat up in a hospital bed didn't sit well with him, which is why he had called the shot. Work at the office served as a distraction from it all.

Even so, work came with its own line of aggravation as he responded to emails from other companies trying to write out contracts for business with Lil Dread and another artist on his roster. With Susie as general director, the job was hers, and the messages should have been replied to long ago. With that, he opened the line and dialed Susie's extension.

"Susie, speaking," her voice came over the speaker.

"Good morning, Susie. I'm logged into the business email account, and I'm trying to figure out why am I responding to -month-old business offers?"

There was no immediate reply.

"Hello?" Ken said.

"Oh, yes, Mr. Griffith. I sincerely apologize. I've been so busy making sure the dates and deadlines for Lil Dread's tour is on sche-"

Ken took the call off speaker and snatched up the phone. "Susie, you know I hate those weak ass excuses. My emolument to you has nothing to do with setting dates or none of that shit. That's his manager's job! Since you don't understand your job description, I'll explain. I pay you to ensure that everybody else is doing what I pay them to do and to stay on top of the email account for possible offers. If dates aren't right, that means you need to be on his manager's ass like the green on grass. Force them to work harder."

"I understand," she said humbly.

"Listen, Susie. I'll finish this up. I'm going to leave some paperwork with my assistant that requires your signature. I won't be in much longer. Please don't let this happen again."

"Yes, sir, I promise you it won't."

CHAPTER 6

"It's been almost a year, son." Melvin Rogers, better known as Pops, was a fat old man, fifty to be exact. He stood 5'5" with light brown skin and a face covered with scars, pimples, and ugly blemishes. He rocked a graying three-inch afro. He and his son, Mike, were in the kitchen, seated at the heavy-duty cherry wood table that he'd built over twenty years ago. They were drinking beer.

Pops was also the father of Jon Rogers, the seventeen-year-old who was fatally murdered along with his pregnant girlfriend about a year ago. Pops had been close to Jon, closer than he and Mike would ever be. Jon had told him about the burglary he'd planned on the cousin's stash house, and he broke bread with Pops and Mike after pulling it off.

Street wit told Pops that J-Bo and Flip were responsible for the murders, but he had no solid proof. He and Mike would have been attempted to kill the duo, but they were apprehended too fast, and then the news verified what they thought they already knew.

"And Rika," Pops' voice was softer than before, "was gonna give me my first grandbaby."

"We can't let this shit ride, Pops." Mike was hurting still. He sipped his 2-11. "I just wanna smoke one of them fuck niggas." He felt really bad for not avenging his little brother's death. When the homicide detective woke them up that late night to deliver the bad news, they didn't know how to take it. They were beyond heartbroken. Mike didn't think he would make it beyond that point. He and Jon were so close; he just wanted to be wherever his brother was. He tried to take his own life, but the gun was on safety, and Pops eventually talked him out of doing it.

Mike and Pops looked like twins, except Mike's haircut was low, and he was twenty years younger. Pops definitely understood his son's pain, but he also understood reality.

He took a deep breath. "Mike, you know I understand, but we can't."

"Why not? Why can't I just go wet one of them nigga's up, huh?"

Is he stupid or what? Pops wondered. "How the hell you gonna do that with them in jail, Mike? And how we know if it was really them? Yea, it looks like it was them, but how do we really know?"

"Pops, you know damn well it was J-Bo 'nem!" he screamed, mad as hell. "Jon took them folks' shit, and bout seven months later, he and Rika get gunned down. Then J-Bo 'nem get booked the same night for it. C'mon man. I know what tha fuck goin' on." He downed his beer and popped another tab. He couldn't believe his father was saying some shit like this. He was wondering if his dad was retarded or something.

"Ok, fuck it. What you wanna do, Mike? What can we do?" He sat all the way back in his chair and crossed his arms, wanting his son to know there was nothing they could do at this point.

Mike downed his third beer for the afternoon. "Find the family."

Pops sighed and sipped his Heineken. He hadn't expected the boy to take this route. "Let me make a few calls."

****

Dr. Rasool entered the room. "Ms. Waters." His tone was warm as he approached the sleeping woman.

Nae woke, stretching and yawning. "Is everything alright, Doc?"

"Everything is fine, Ms. Waters," he ensured. "I'm going to prescribe you something for pain. If you take one tab in the morning with breakfast and one before bed, you'll catch the pains before they come, and you won't feel a thing." He smiled.

"So, am I being released?" she yawned again.

"Yes, but," he gave her a stern stare like a father does his teenage daughter. "You need to rest. It's very important that you take it easy for an entire week. No working. No raising your voice. No cooking because you have to be on your feet too long. Just relax and allow the swelling to go down more," he instructed.

She giggled. It didn't hurt as much that time. "I'll take it easy, Doc."

"Alright, I'll go print out you're release papers, write out your prescription, and you'll be good to go." He walked out.

It was 11:10 a.m. when she looked at her cell phone. She dialed Ken up.

"Hello?" he answered.

"Um, hey, it's Nae." She wasn't expecting him to answer so quickly.

"Yea, I know who it is. How are you?"

"I'm being released."

"I'll be there in thirty."

They ended the call, and there was a shallow knock at the door. "Who is it? I mean, come in," she called out. She was discombobulated, knowing Dr. Rasool usually would walk right in.

It was Detective Walker. "Good morning, Ms. Waters."

"Good morning, Detective." She couldn't wait for him to tell her that Nick was in custody so she could press charges on his ass.

"I'm here to update you on the status of my investigation." He checked out her face in silence, seeing the swelling has gone down just a bit. "I didn't find Mr. Taylor physically." She was instantly disappointed. "But I did find him in our database, and I quickly issued a warrant for his arrest." He glanced around the room. "His phone goes straight to voicemail. Has he contacted you since the incident? Reached out to you in any way?"

"No." She was going to tell him about the call from Mario but decided not to.

"Okie dokie, I'll keep in touch. I won't stop until he's in prison, serving at least ten mandatory years. If he contacts you in any type of way, contact me, and we'll set him up. Ok?" He handed her his business card, hoping she wasn't the type that would soon fall victim to Nick's "I'm sorry" pleas.

She nodded.

Detective Walker left, and Dr. Rasool returned with a yellow sheet of paper and a blue card.

"Sign by the x." He laid the paper on the portable table before her. Nae signed it. He examined her signature, tore off a copy for her to keep, and kept the other two for hospital records. "Here's your prescription." He handed her the card. "You have a ride home?"

"Yes, they're on the way."

"Very well, you're all ready to go." Right when he left out, she received a text from Ken.

I'm five minutes away, Beautiful. Be ready.

The nurse brought her a fresh gown to wear. Her bloody clothes were being used as evidence to convict Nick. She requested a toothbrush and toothpaste. By the time she finished tightening up, Ken was texting that he was turning in the hospital's parking lot.

****

The restaurant was live, bright, and teaming with important-looking people. The sound of people talking, orders being taken, and silverware meeting plates were all to be heard; and the smell of buttered oven rolls and freshly seasoned steak filled the air.

"What will you two gentlemen be having today?" It was a skinny brunette who questioned the two men seated at one of the tables in her waiting area. They were at Million Dollar Steaks, one of the most expensive and best quality steakhouses in the south. One meal could easily cost a minimum wage worker's weekly pay. With that, it was a place for the upper class. The two men at the table were District Attorney Billy Anderson and his fairly new assistant, William White. Billy Anderson was a heavy-set Caucasian male with a bald head and a long pointy nose. He's been the county's DA for the past twenty years. Mr. William was also Caucasian, blonde hair, blue eyes, and was a lot younger than Billy. He'd just completed law school and was still learning the ropes. But he was very familiar with fucking people over. He'd already handled a few small cases on his own, but since being hired by Atlanta and partnered with crooked ass Billy Anderson, he's definitely been learning all the things you're not supposed to do as a district attorney.

"I'll take a five-pounder," Billy ordered. "Medium rare and white wine, please."

The waitress jotted his order down and looked at William.

"I'll have the same, with root beer instead of wine."

She scribbled on her notepad once more and looked from Billy to William. “Got it. Would that be all for the two of you?”

“Yes, that would be all,” Billy said.

She smiled. “Okay, great. Two five pounders, medium-rare coming right up.” She turned and walked off.

Billy frowned upon his partner’s preference. He didn’t like the fact that William didn’t drink any form of alcohol.

“So,” Billy unbuttoned his jacket suit. “How do you feel about the Dew’s?”

“We offered forty, do thirty,” William said.

“I already knew they would deny it because it’s high as hell. Plus, they think they’re smart asses, right?”

William nodded in agreement with his subordinate.

“So, we go to trial. Of course, they’ll lose, and they’ll get life without parole. I may even seek the death penalty. What do you think?” Billy smiled. His teeth were so perfect, William could tell they were veneers.

“I prefer life without,” William asserted. “Death is the easy way out. Let’s make the niggers suffer.”

“Yes!” Billy exclaimed, and they toasted.

“To the Dew’s.” Billy liked his young partner’s way of thinking. At first, he thought he would have to speak to someone about switching William because he seemed too uptight, too lame, and by the book.

He’s coming around just fine, Billy thought.

Neither of the two liked black people or anyone that spoke Spanish as their primary language. *If you’re not white, you’ll lose the fight,* was Billy’s favorite quote.

William inherited racism from his grandparents. Billy, on the other hand, had experienced it firsthand. They ate as much as their stomachs would allow then Billy paid the $310 tab.

****

"Heyyy, sis." Diamond said through her end, always happy to talk to Nae.

"Hey, baby. I was released this morning."

"I wanted to come and see you so bad, but these security people were trippin' something serious."

Nae laughed. "It's ok. What you doing, girl?"

"I was watching a movie. I'm just sitting here looking crazy now." They both laughed. "You?"

"Lying in bed, just got out the shower. Girl, his house is big as fuck," she whispered, not wanting him to hear that.

"He took a shower with you?"

"No, he's taking one now. I want to see you, though." She changed the subject before Diamond could start talking nasty.

"They just told me this morning I can have visits today and the day after for two hours apiece."

"I thought it was only on the weekends, though?"

"Girl, they switch shit up so fucking much, ugh. But just let me know which day you want to come."

"Ask them if l can bring Ken, too. And we can't come both days?" Nae thought it was strange because she would usually go see her sister as much as they would allow.

"Yea, you can bring him. They don't care about that. And, hell nah, you can't come both days, girl. Garrett has been tripping. I gotta call me some dick over here."

Nae burst out laughing. "Girl, you are a mess. And when I bring his fine ass, you bet not be on no extra shit." She warned. "But we'll come tomorrow, girl. Love you." She hung up.

I can get used to this shit, she thought, laying in his California king-sized bed, peering around the sprucely furnished room. There were thick black and gold drapes on the windows, obscuring the sun from her delicate face. He had two 72" flat screen TVs mounted side by side on the wall. The wood bed railing had gold trimming on the outer layer, black on the inner. There was a big gold and black dresser with a thick, black and white Louis V. carpet laid across it with a full-length mirror on top of it. She wore a small YBE t-shirt, and a black pair of Victoria's Secret set that he picked up for her on the way back from the hospital. She was impressed how he wasn't ashamed to walk right in and purchase her an underwear set.

Ken came from the bathroom wearing nothing but a pair of green and grey Ralph Lauren polo boxers that hugged his waist snugly. His print was easily seen. His dreads hung wildly, and his brown skin shined from the coat of baby oil he'd applied.

Oh my god, she thought, staring at his entire tatted body, mostly admiring his six-pack. *This nigga is so sexy.*

Nae wanted to fuck, and she could tell by the look in his eyes, he wanted to fuck just as bad.

"Be gentle, baby. My body hurts," she crooned, getting completely naked. "I want it," she purred, once his boxers hit the floor, exposing his thickness. He walked towards her slowly, not saying a word. Even with the bruises on her stomach and chest area from where Nick kicked her, she was still sexy as hell. He was very gentle when spreading her legs. He stared at her clitoris for a few seconds, thinking how pretty and perfect it seemed before he started sucking on it.

"Umm, hmm, ah, Ken," she moaned, already ready to cum. He ate her for a few minutes. He liked the feeling of her pulling on his hair and trying to push his face away when the feeling got too intense. She seemed to not be able to take any more of his professional tongue, and he climbed on top of her. He looked into her eyes as he began to slide into her body.

She grabbed his dick. "Wait, you don't have a condom?"

Ken looked at her. He thought he didn't need one, feeling as though they had built a little trust. "Yea, I'll get one."

"No, it's ok." She moved her hand for him to enter her, and he did, sliding in balls deep. Her left hand was full of his bedding and her right hand full of his hair as he delivered slow but deep strokes to her soaking pussy. She moaned, screamed, scratched his back, pulled his hair, and came several times. Looking around the room, she felt like she was a queen somewhere on an island with nobody but her king. His breathing and strokes both accelerated before he pulled out and came all over his blanket.

Looking at his thick load, she thought, *I would've swallowed it.*

He kissed her sore lips really softly before scooting down. She thought he was getting up to go to the bathroom, but his head stopped between her legs and started sucking on her clit again.

"I want to taste it on my tongue, Nae," he whispered, flicking his tongue fast, slow, faster, slower, fast again, slow again.

"Aaahh, Ken, baby!" she grabbed his hair once more as she felt herself reaching climax again. "Aaahh, baby. I'm cumming. Oh, my God, I'm cumming!"

"I want it on my tongue, Nae." He sped up the flicks of his tongue as she came. Her body quivered this time. He swallowed her fluids, thinking of how sweet she tasted.

CHAPTER 7

Pops and Mike met up at IHOP and were enjoying some cheesecake pancakes and crispy fried bacon. They sat at the last table in the back, closest to the window, so Pops could monitor all movement inside and outside the restaurant. He was a vigilant old man, and he knew the spot he'd chosen; no one could eavesdrop. Pops had called for this meeting this morning, letting Mike know that he had something to tell him.

"So, what's up?" Mike asked.

"I made a few calls to the street." He took a forkful of pancakes.

Mike was staring at his father, hoping he would chew a little bit faster. He was thirsty for answers, badly wanting to whack somebody about Jon and Rika.

He threw his hands up, growing impatient. "And what did the streets tell you?"

Why the fuck is he talking so goddamn much? Pops thought. He took his precious time washing the food down with a few sips of the delicious orange juice.

"Hello?" Mike waved his hand.

Pops looked around the restaurant, then back at his son. "Michael, just shut the fuck up!" he snapped in a muffled voice with a finger pointing in Mike's face. From the look Mike was making, Pops knew he felt like he was stalling him out on purpose. Not giving a damn, Pops took another bite, chewed slowly, swallowed, looked around the restaurant again, and took another sip of his juice. "I didn't find anything on any family of his, but," he paused when the girl came to refill their drinks and ask if they needed anything else. They didn't. "I got a little info on a close friend of J-Bo's. My resources say he's a businessman." Mike wasn't touching his food. He only sat there like a sponge, soaking in everything his father was saying. “I don’t have an address on him, but I hear he has an office, right here in Atlanta. The only problem is, he’s plugged. His name really holds weight.”

Mike sucked his teeth, finally dropping his gaze and biting into his pancakes. Once he sipped his juice, he almost choked, trying to talk at the same time. “What da hell you mean, he plugged? Nigga, we plugged!” he was heated.

Two elderly white women that were seated a few seats up looked back at them.

“Hey, hey, hey, hey. Lower yo fuckin’ voice, stupid ass lil nigga.”

Mike glanced at the two old nosy bitches, then leaned into the table, getting closer to Pops. “We hold weight, too, Pops. What da hell you talking ‘bout? I feel like you tryna belittle our street credit.”

“They say he’s Lil Dread’s owner,” Pops said.

Mike frowned. “Shawty dat rap? And what da hell you mean his owner?”

“I meant to say he signed Lil Dread to his label. And the street gang YoungBoss, he’s the head honcho.”

Mike was familiar with the entertainment label YoungBoss. Also, with the opulent amount of ruthless street niggas that claimed it as their gang.

“Of course, our name holds weight,” Pops went on. “But not like this. The wrong move could easily turn us into dead men. Don’t forget what happened the last time you got into it with one of those YoungBoss niggas. It cost me a lot of money to stop that beef, Michael. We gon’ move smart this time.”

“So, this friend of J-Bo’s is over them nigga’s we had that issue with?”

Pops nodded.

"But how can we be dead men when he's some type of office work doing mothafucka?" he asked, clearly ignoring what Pops had previously said about the gang.

Pops gobbled down the last of his bacon. "Smoke in the mirrors, Son. I did my homework. He's a beast. They say killing is his favorite game."

"Shiid, mines too. Let tha games begin." Mike smiled.

Pops snapped his fingers in Mike's face, snatching him out of whatever he was thinking. "No, sir. I'm running this show, do you understand me?"

Mike took a deep breath before slouching in his chair. His mind was racing a million miles per hour. "Yea, so what's the plan?"

"I don't know yet, but I'll figure it out," he stood and pulled out his wallet. "Until then, just keep doing what you're doing now. Just sitting around looking stupid." He put thirty dollars on the table before leaving.

****

Ken admired Nae's petite body as the hot water sleuthed into every crease and over every curve. Even bruised and battered, she was still a dime. Gently washing her skin, he thought of how he'd definitely allowed this whole ordeal to go too far. She turned to face him so he could get her front side and her smile warmed his insides. She opened her arms for his hard body, and he gladly accepted her embrace. Snuggling in his arms, she wished she could assume that same position forever. He rubbed his hand across her soft butt cheeks before squeezing one.

"Um," she moaned softly when he used a finger to flick her clit. She looked up into his eyes and could clearly see the love he had for her. She wondered if he could see it in her eyes as well. If she spoke the words, would he say them back? Would he deny what she could clearly see? Her mind raced.

He slid one finger in her tight walls from the back. She bit down on his muscular chest, and that got his dick rock hard. Softly, he kissed her healing lips before sliding his tongue in her mouth. Pulling back, she turned, bent over, and gripped the gold railing mounted in marble. He slid in, slowly, finding a steady pace.

"Give it to me, baby," she moaned, making him feel mightier than he already did. Her little round, yellow ass jiggled and jiggled as he piped her more and more. Escalating his speed, she moaned louder and louder. She looked back at him. The sight alone could make any man bust a nut. She could tell he was about to cum again so soon because she could feel him speeding up and breathing hard. The only thing that could be heard was skin slapping, heavy breathing, and highly pleasurable moans from both of them. With hopes of him being reckless and releasing in her, she used all the strength in her body to throw it back. He pulled out and exploded on her pretty butt cheeks.

"Kenneth, I can't take it anymore," she turned to face him. "I have to tell you something."

He silenced her with a finger to her lips. He had a feeling she was about to say she loved him. He wasn't ready to hear it. "Let's just wash up and get dressed, baby." He hoped she would be a good girl and not pursue the topic.

****

I'ma kill the office work doing mothafucka, myself, Mike thought, sitting in his room on his laptop. He'd pulled up a picture of Ken on Google. Pops had finally revealed the name of the man that he was speaking of earlier. He looked at J-Bo and Flip's mugshot that was glued to the side of his computer, which he'd printed out months ago. "And you two bitch-ass niggas."

Mike prayed every night that the duo would beat the case and be liberated, so he and Pops could rob them of their lives. As far as him handling Ken, that plan was vague, but he refused to throw in the towel. Even if he had a chance to kill Ken today, he still wouldn't be satisfied. His thirst for vengeance wouldn't fully be quenched until he got the cousins, or the closest thing to them: mama, daddy, brother, sister, son, daughter, grandmamma, granddaddy, or baby mama.

****

Having gotten the authorized clearance, Nae left the reception desk and made her way through the Sheraton Hotel's grand lobby with Ken at her side. She answered her ringing phone, listened, then said, "We're coming up now, baby."

Ken sported a pair of white Levi's, a tailored Prada dress shirt, eggshell in color, and a white pair of Prada boots with gold trimming, matching his $20,000 gold, diamond-encrusted Rolex. Nae had offered to braid his dreads, but he decided to let them hang and dry.

Nae was in a $6,000 outfit bought by Ken from Saks Fifth Avenue, a skintight Prada dress along with a pair of white and gold Prada slides.

The elevator was all gold, had a digital screen and no buttons.

"This place seems really nice." She smiled.

"Nice, isn't it?" Nae asked.

Ken nodded. "I've been here once before."

"You have?" Nae asked.

"A business meeting," Ken lied, having been there on multiple occasions with several different women.

"Did you enjoy the stay?"

He nodded, trying not to think of the model he fucked on the elevator during his last visit.

Two male guards were standing there when the doors slid open. A big lumberjack-looking man with a red beard and his skinny partner with a crew cut and trimmed mustache walked inside. Both were white, in normal clothes, and armed with radios and pistols. The third story was private and only *permitted* people could get off there. Nae's clearance had to come from the reception desk, through ID verification at the front desk, and further confirmation from the guards here. Only then was the digital restriction removed by way of computer.

"Sir," Lumberjack came forward. "You need to undergo a routine search before you're allowed in the room."

Ain't this bout a bitch, Ken thought, looking to Nae, who wore an apologetic expression. He was glad to have left his strap in the car. *Good thing I'm not strapped.*

Ken stepped to the wall, on which he placed both his hands. Lumberjack positioned himself behind him while Crew Cut stood watching.

Lumberjack tapped Ken's heel with the tip of his foot. "Spread your legs."

Ken did so reluctantly and was frisked from shoulder to ankles, thinking of how much J-Bo was going to compensate him for the humiliation suffered.

Lumberjack finished and Ken stepped away from the wall, readjusting his collar.

"Your turn." Lumberjack was looking past Ken at Nae.

Ken positioned himself protectively in front of Nae. His eyes narrowed. The idea didn't sit well with him. "You're not patting her down."

Crew Cut took a defensive stance, placing his hand on the butt of his nine. "It's either he pats her down, or she doesn't go in."

Ken looked to Crew Cut. "Or we can se-"

"It's ok, baby," Nae put a hand on Ken's shoulder, cutting him off before things got out of control. "It's protocol." Nae put her hands on the wall, and Lumberjack smiled. He positioned himself behind her and began a routine pat-down while Ken watched gritting his teeth the whole time.

Ken shook his head. *All this cause a bitch wanna tell? Police-ass-bitch!*

Lumberjack finished, and Crew Cut spoke into his radio. "They're clean."

Ken was glaring at Lumberjack.

"Can we go, now?" Nae asked.

Lumberjack nodded.

Nae grabbed Ken by the arm and headed down the hall. At the door, they were searched again before being granted access to the suite.

"Oh, my God!" Diamond squealed, rushing Nae for a hug "Aww," she said, rubbing gently on Nae's bruises.

Really? Ken thought. He couldn't believe this pretty little bitch was causing such a big problem. He would certainly kill her when the time was right. He noted how much she and Nae favored; they were almost twins.

"This is my man, Ken." Nae pointed to him. "Ken, this is my little sister, Dasha, but everybody calls her Diamond."

Ken smiled and gave her a one-armed hug.

"How are you?" he asked, not giving a fuck.

"I'm fine." Diamond pulled back from their hug. "I'll be better whenever I can get me some front row tickets to see Lil Dread's lil fine ass," she joked.

"That's all?" He faked a smile. "I can let you meet the lil homie."

"That's what's up. So, everybody who be screaming YBE in their songs, you know all of them?"

He laughed. "Yea, it's my label."

"So, you the shot caller?" she smiled.

"Yea, I do the hiring and the firing."

That made the girls laugh. They took seats on the bed, and Ken relaxed on the couch as the girls chatted away and brought each other up to date on local events. Ken sat in silence.

On several occasions, Diamond caught Ken staring at her, assuming it was in a manner of sexual interest. She was loyal to her sister, but if he wanted to, she definitely would fuck him.

Ken was silently debating whether to make a financial offer to Diamond or to simply go with his first mind and dome check the stupid bitch. For all the trouble, he leaned towards the latter. Considering his regards for Nae, however, the prospect of offering money wasn't out of the question. With the fact Nae could in no way be made aware of a sinister plot against her sister, nor could Ken even hope to have her involved with the actual plot to do so, murking the dumb bitch would prove to be the more difficult route. Hell, she was up to her pretty ass with security. A nigga needs clearance to even get on her fucking floor! With that, a financial offer was further considered.

Ken locked eyes with Diamond, breaking contact the moment he saw the lust within.

"Baby," Nae asked. Are you okay?"

The question caught him off guard, but his response was quick. "I'm good. Just contemplating some issues at the office."

Satisfied with his reply, Nae picked up where she left off with her sister.

CHAPTER 8

"Baby, I'm really sorry. Baby, I just snapped." Slick Nick took a deep breath as he thought of what more to say to Nae's voicemail, something he hadn't said already.

"Nae, I know I went too far, but let's just work past that, okay? I love you."

He hung up. Calling right back was on his mind, but he decided against it. He'd been calling and texting her all day to no avail. He shook his head, unwilling to accept that it was over.

Nick was parked in an empty Krispy Kreme parking lot in the West End. It was dark and other than an abandoned Buick, his car was the only one there. The doughnut and coffee shop were closed for the night, but here is where Chingy had wanted to meet when he'd called to buy another half.

Where the fuck is this fool? he thought. *And why in hell he wanna meet here anyway?* He wondered. He called Chingy again for the third time and got no answer. In a year of dealing with the man, this was the first time he'd asked to meet somewhere different, and that didn't sit well with him.

"Man, what tha fuck!" He was more than irritated, knowing the police would be lurking in the streets in the wee hours of the night. He was ready to get his shit and get back to his neck of the woods.

****

Chingy rode past Queen City Strip Club and swung his Camry swiftly into Krispy Kreme's parking lot with no turn signal. He whipped around and backed in beside Slick Nick's vehicle, preparing for a quick exit when the time came to smash out. He peeped the scene, and everything seemed safe.

With that, he gripped Takia tightly before opening his door and stepping out of the car.

Slick Nick, he thought. *Nothing personal, bro, but the shot was called.*

****

Ken and Nae were in his bed together, laughing as they watched reruns of *Martin.* Which, as Ken discovered, was her favorite show. Though his eyes were on the screen, and he shared her laughter, his internal conflict was prevalent: how was he to deal with Diamond? There was the thought of straight knocking her ass the fuck off, and there was J-Bo's suggestion with the bribe.

There were aspects to either approach that complicated matters.

If he were to make a proposal to Diamond, to which she refused and reported to her sister, it would expose everything down to his chance meeting with Nae in her shop. If by some means, Diamond did accept the offer and its condition, he couldn't see her keeping the secret. They were too close. He saw proof of that tonight at the hotel.

"Something bothering you?" Nae had her head on Ken's chest, looking up at him.

Ken looked down at her. "Huh?"

"Is something bothering you? One minute you were laughing, the next minute you were zoned out."

He gave a weak smile. "Just preparing myself mentally for an upcoming business proposal. Nothing serious."

Ken's phone rang on his nightstand. He grabbed it up and looked at the screen. It was a weird 800 number that he knew could only be J-Bo calling from the County.

Speaking of the devil, Ken thought. He listened to the voice prompt then answered. “Yo.”

“Aye, Ken, wassup?”

“Oh, hey, how are you?”

“I’m aiight. How dat business goin’?”

“Oh, everything is great, Sir.”

J-Bo paused. Ken only used that tone and voice with him when the setting wasn’t right for certain conversations. With it close to eleven, he decided to press. “You in ya office or sum, big bruh?”

“No, sir, I’m not. Give me one second, please.” He stood up. “Excuse me, baby girl. This is business that can’t wait.”

“Okay.” She nodded and gave her attention back to the television. There was a good episode that she hadn’t seen, and she wasn’t trying to miss one bit of it.

He kissed her on the forehead and got out the bed. Throwing on some black Nike basketball shorts, he made his way downstairs to the dark kitchen. “What’s up, J-Bo?”

“Just ready to come home. How dat shit goin?”

Ken peeped around the corner to see if Nae had followed. She hadn’t; her eyes were glued to his 72-inch TV.

“Everything is in motion, bro. I met her for the first time today.” He peeped around the corner at the stairs. “You know she’s in that program shit, so I know what to do. I’ll do it next time I see her.”

“That’s what da fuck I’m talking ‘bout, nigga!” J-Bo was excited. “But look, bro, I’m finna hit da shower. It’s almost lockdown time. I just wanted to touch bases wit’cha on that. I ain’t doubtin’ you or nothin’ like that. It’s just…you know.”

“Yea, Bro…I know. But aiight, cool. Love you, bro. Handle ya business. I got this.”

“Fa’sho.”

Ken hung up, went back upstairs, and climbed in bed with Nae.

"I missed you." She snuggled back up under him.

I missed you, too." He kissed her.

"Did your business talk go well?" She secretly wondered what business it could've been near to eleven o'clock at night, but she didn't push the issue, thinking it too early to be showing signs of insecurity.

He grinned. "It went great."

****

"It's about damn time," Slick Nick said as Chingy swung into the lot. He'd grown impatient with the wait but had given his undivided attention to some local hoes that were trying to start up a new twerk team on Instagram. He put his phone down, oblivious to the fact Chingy was parking in reverse but curious as to why he was in a cheap ass Toyota Camry.

He smiled through his window. "What's good, my nigga?" The night's air smelled different for some odd reason. Chingy opened the car door and stood up, standing in his door, scanning the lot. Something about his body language was off. He could never see Chingy crossing him, but he was already at three *nevers:* had never been late, had never changed spots, had never been seen driving that car.

Slick Nick reached to surreptitiously grabbed his nine off the passenger seat, tucking it on his waistline. *Just in case,* he thought, getting out of the car.

****

"Just fuck off," Nae said, having just listened to another of Slick Nick's relentless voicemails. She put her phone down and gave her attention back to her favorite sitcom.

Ken was slightly annoyed; she'd been checking her voicemails all day. He'd said nothing so far, but he was curious about the last comment. "Everything alright?"

"Everything is fine, baby." She put her hand in his, but his expression made her continue. "It's just Nicholas leaving me messages about how sorry he is and shit."

"How do you feel about him?" He chose his words carefully. "And before you respond, make sure you're honest with me." He gave his attention to the TV.

She looked up to the ceiling, then at her hands. "I don't like him. I'm not in love with him, but I do still have love for him as a person. I wouldn't want to see him hurt or anything like that, maybe go to prison. Honestly, I just want him to leave me alone."

He nodded, and they continued to watch *Martin* in silence. All of Nae's feelings mattered to him.

You better thank God, nigga, he thought as he sent Chingy a text telling him to stand down on the hit.

****

Looking around from his car's doorway, Chingy took slow, profound breaths. He'd killed plenty of times before, but he hadn't established a relationship, business, nor personal dealing with the others either. He hated when he had to down people that grew on him over time. He wished there was a way around this. His phone vibrated, notifying him of a text. He ignored it, figuring there was nothing more important than what he was doing.

"What tha hell you ova there playin', hide and seek?" Slick Nick walked around the car to face Chingy. He made it around the whip, and Chingy raised his gun, aiming directly at Nick's chest. Nick's hands went up, heart accelerating, his breathing rapid. "Chingy, what tha fuck?" He knew something was flakey since the phone call.

Chingy ordered him to get back in his car. "And keep ya fuckin' hands up where I can see 'em."

"Aiight, Aiight." Slick Nick turned around and started walking back to his car. "What's this shit about, Chingy? I ain't did nothin' but good business wit' you since day one. Money never came up short. Not one red cent. Talk to me, Bro!"

Chingy's weapon was trained on Slick Nick's back the entire time. The man's name was given to him for a reason. "You just had to pistol-whip a bitch. You a real hoe-ass nigga."

From that, Slick Nick concluded that Chingy was in some way tied to Tisha. As he slid in his driver's seat, he discreetly removed his pistol from his waistband. Unfortunately, Chingy was observant, and he peeped game. He pulled the trigger, and the automatic ripped the night in three quick bursts, bringing pools of red dots to Slick Nick's back, neck, and head as he slumped in the front seat of his car. He gave the parking lot a once over, covered his hands with his sleeve, and ran fast around the front of his car to Slick Nick's driver's side. He shifted the man's car in drive and ran back to hop in behind his own wheel, smashing out as Slick Nick's Chevy rolled out of the parking lot and into the street, dragging his lifeless body to the ground for the coroner to pick up.

CHAPTER 9

Mike was once again at the family's famous Wooden table. He was destroying a big bowl of Cinnamon Toast Crunch as he was surfing the web on his laptop, trying to find something on Ken. Anything! Ken wasn't like the average nigga that gets a little money and starts putting on all super flashy and had everybody in his business; the chances of finding out about his personal life from the internet was minute. With that, he searched Google for the man's place of business and dialed the number provided.

"Young boss offices," the receptionist asked. "How may I direct your call?"

He was trying to swallow a mouthful.

"Hello?" The receptionist repeated.

"Uh, yea, let me holla at Kenneth Griffith."

She paused, thinking if she should hang up or not. "Who's calling?"

"I'm a good friend, shawty. Just put him on the phone."

"Well, Mr. Griffith isn't in right now. Would you like to leave a message?"

"Yea, I got a message. Tell dat pussy-ass nigga he dead meat! I'ma kill him and all his homeboys! I'ma-" The receptionist hung up, cutting him off.

"I'ma kill dat fuck nigga!" Mike jumped to his feet and smacked the big bowl from the table. It struck the floor and shattered everywhere.

Pops heard the ruckus from his room, and tip-toed to the kitchen with his .38 special in hand, ready to off some shit. Mike was standing there looking like a madman. Cereal, milk, and glass all over the floor the floor. Pops glanced at the laptop.

Pops pocketed the revolver. "What the hell are you doing, Mike?"

"I'ma kill all dem niggas!" Mike's voice was thunderous. "Real nigga shit!"

Pops approached him and firmly gripped his shoulders. "Son, what did I tell you? Just wait until I get some more info."

"Get da fuck off me!" He jerked away and stormed out the front door.

"Mike!" Pops called after his son. "Wait…." He ran out onto the porch. "Michael, yo stupid ass gonna get killed. Just chill the fuck out!"

Mike ignored Pops and continued to his car. He got in, cranked it up, and burnt rubber down the street.

"Fuck!" Pops watched the car disappear up the street. He went back inside, shaking his head as he closed the door. Unable to sit, he paced the living room floor as he attempted to regain control of emotions that spiraled out of control. The death of his wife to the car accident that he survived, the loss of his youngest son to the street was a lot for one person to handle.

Pops punched the wall, leaving a crushed impression in the sheetrock. Why wouldn't his boys take heed? He had raised them. Had been in their lives since birth. Wasn't it likely he knew what was best for them, having been in the game far longer? Pops had told Jon to take his baby mama and leave town for at least a year after he found out who's spot that he'd hit. That was a week before he was murdered in cold blood. It pissed him off to know how hardheaded his sons were. Mike was moving way too fast for his own good. If Pops didn't intervene and do so quickly, he would be picking a casket for his second son.

****

"Yep, just like that." Nae was instructing Tisha with a new hairstyle. "Then you let her tips sit in boiling water for twenty seconds, and you're done."

Practice makes perfect, and practice with hair could only come from hands-on experience. With that, the hairdo was free to those who allowed Tisha to gain the necessary hands-on experience. Tisha had done four heads today, all of whom had no complaints with the job done.

Even though the doctor had prescribed rest and no work, Nae had insisted that Ken take her home, let her change, and drop her off to her car and to work. Ken had sided with the doctor's orders but had relented at her persistence and promise to work light and off her feet.

And true to her word, Nae was relaxed in a chair next to Tisha and her present client.

Tisha smiled appreciatively. "Oh, thank you, girl."

"You know I got you." Nae went back to the pages of her *Women's Health* magazine.

"How are you today, Ms. Waters?"

The voice was familiar, and Nae raised her head to find Detective Walker there before her. She rose to shake his hand, and it was something about the look on his face that said something unexpected was on the table. She knew something wasn't right. "I'm fine, Detective. Did you find him?"

Walker studied her a moment before looking similarly at Tisha, then at the remaining two women in the salon. Nae shared a curious glance with Tisha, who shrugged.

"Ms. Waters?" Detective Walker took out his pen and pad. "Where were you between ten and eleven pm last night?"

"Umm, I was at my boyfriend's house in Decatur." She was nervous all of a sudden.

He wrote it all down, and before she could ask what the problem was, he fired another question. “Ms. Waters, when was the last time you spoke to Mr. Taylor?”

“The same day that he came in here and beat my ass.”

“Ms. Waters, I don’t have time for your little nasty-ass attitude. Nor do I have time for games or lies. I need honest answers to every question I ask. Do you understand?” He was very frank. That changed her view; it felt graver now. Tisha and the other women got up and walked out.

Nae’s heartbeat raced faster as her brow creased in confusion. “Detective, what’s going on?”

He held his hand up. “You and Mr. Taylor were on the phone at 10:10 last night.” He flipped a page in his notepad. “That call lasted for three minutes. The same length as the call from 9:00, I’m quite curious to know what the two of you were talking about.”

“Detective, um,” she had to find her words. “I never talked to Nick. I sent him to voicemail, and he left really long messages.”

“What was he saying in the messages?”

She shrugged her shoulders. “The average, I love you, I’m sorry bullshit.”

“Ok, I’ll be in touch.” He turned to leave.

“Wait!” Nae called out.

Walker turned.

“What’s going on?”

“Ms. Waters, when I came to see you in the hospital, I was taking a few cases off the hands of another detective. I usually don’t take cases like that. I’m a homicide detective. Last night, Nicholas Taylor, AKA Slick Nick, was found dead in the West End.”

****

At his office, Ken scrolled through his phone, searching for Diamond's phone number that he'd taken from Nae's phone last night while she was asleep. He wasn't the type to snoop through a woman's phone. However, he couldn't ask for the number and expect Nae not to demand solid answers, which is the last thing he needed.

What would be Diamond's reply? he wondered, dialing Diamond's number from his office line.

"Hello?" she answered groggily.

"Good morning, Diamond. It's Nae's boyfriend, Ken. Is this a good time? I need to speak to you about something."

"Hold up."

He could hear her moving around.

"Ken?" she sounded more awake now.

"Yes, I'm here."

"Um, ok. What's up?"

He got comfortable in his big rolling chair. "Listen, I'm fully aware of your situation, and it's very clear that I'm not the only one."

"What are you talking about, Ken?"

"The two guys that you're testifying on; their family reached out to me a few minutes ago." His fingers were locked, his thumbs twirling around each other. "Because I'm a very resourceful man, they asked for my assistance to find the witness… and that just so happens to be you." He paused to let that sink in before continuing.

There was a knock at the office door before it swung open, and Susie's head popped in. He held his hand up, and she left just as quickly as she appeared.

"Quite a coincidence the way things work, huh? But the point is that they are offering you fifty-thousand dollars in cash money for you not to testify."

"How do you know their family, Ken?" she asked skeptically.

"They own a distribution company that I have a few contracts with."

"Do you know the men I'm testifying on?"

"No, I'm just relaying a proposition, but I think it's a sweet deal. I mean, free money, right?"

"Yea, it is, but what they did to those kids was wrong. Their families need justice, and it's on my heart to give it to them."

Ken took a deep breath, releasing a heavy sigh. "I fully understand. I'll just pretend I never spoke to you if they ask."

"Ok, and don't forget my backstage passes to see Lil Dread."

"OK, I got you. And hey, do me a favor, keep this conversation between us. I don't want your sister to know about it."

"Okay. No worries. I got you."

"Cool. Take care."

"Uh-huh. You, too." She hung up.

Ken bowed his head and closed his eyes, his dreads falling about his face. He gripped the bridge of his nose and prayed that it didn't have to go the way he had thought it might. He really didn't want to kill Diamond. He would much rather pay her, but if he was put in the position with no other choice, he would definitely knock her noodles loose.

Ken dialed Susie's extension and told her to come back.

"Hey," he greeted when she came through the door.

"Hello, there." She took a seat in front of his desk. "This morning, someone called for you. After being asked to leave a message, this was all he could get out before Khloe hung up on him." Susie handed him a single sheet of paper with the typed message.

Look, shawty. Tell that pussy nigga he dead meat. I'ma kill him and all his homeboys.

Ken frowned.

"I thought that was very disturbing, so I did a full trace on that number." She pointed to the name on the page.

"Michael Rogers." Ken sat back, tossed the paper on his desk, and shrugged. "I'm not sure who that could've been."

"I think you need a bodyguard. We can definitely afford it."

"Hell no! Could've been a prank caller."

"Okay. Okay. Fine. Just watch your back." She stood, and Ken watched her as she made her way to the door.

The prank caller was gone from his mind, so too was the call with Diamond, replaced now with how nicely shaped Susie's ass is for a white girl.

Her black slacks hugged her curves. Her white casual dress shirt looked like it was made to wrap around her small breast.

She was twenty-four years old with short blonde hair, a healthy petite build, and the sexiest pair of cold blue eyes.

"Are you wearing tighter pants?" Ken called after her.

Susie turned at the door. "Why do you ask?"

He got up and approached stealthily. Once there, he rubbed his tongue against her neck. She let out a soft moan, and he reached to lock the door.

"Take those off." He tugged at her pants and started to undo his Gucci belt.

"You gonna fuck me good, boss man?"

She got naked, and he did just that.

CHAPTER 10

J-Bo and Flip were both on their bunks, laid on their backs. J-Bo was staring straight up at the picture of the new Aventador that was just released. He'd ripped the page out of a magazine and taped it to the top of his bunk so he could see it all the time. Flip's eyes were closed. They both had thoughts of freedom.

Flip was twisting his nappy afro. "So, Ken says he done met da bitch already, huh?"

"Hell yea." J-Bo nodded. "Shawty say we should be Gucci real soon."

J-Bo tried to sound like he wasn't worried, but in all actuality, he was. He was the type that would worry about shit outside of his control, while Flip, on the other hand, would just go with the flow. J-Bo felt like things wouldn't go right unless he was able to do them himself, and in this situation, he couldn't do jack shit but put all of his trust into Ken. He most certainly trusted Ken, but with him and his younger cousin's life on the line, he still wished there was more he could do.

J-Bo's thoughts shifted to Shakeena and her baby. He still loved her but was heartbroken by her absence after so long. Her tears and weak-ass excuses weren't good enough for him. He thought it over much, and the time frame did add up to where the baby could be his, but he wasn't claiming a baby when the claim wasn't one hundred. He took a trip to the medical floor last week to get his blood drawn and was anxious for the results.

The dormitory entrance door popped, and an officer stuck his head in. "Jerome Dew! Report to the door fully dressed with a pen!"

Flip sat up. "You expectin' a visit or sumthin?"

"Hell naw." J-Bo sat up and slid on his slides. He stood up, looking for a pen, but Flip was already holding one out for him with a smile on his face. He grabbed it. "Keep tellin' yo ugly ass 'bout bleedin' all my pens out writin' all of them whack ass raps and shit nigga."

Flip laughed. "Whatever, nigga."

In the hallway, the mail officer stood there with a cart beside him. J-Bo knew then that he had legal mail. When he saw all of the other manila envelopes, that was usually the only time the mailroom officer would come up there.

"Mr. Dew, you have certified mail you must sign for." He pointed to the highlighted "X" on a roster sheet. J-Bo signed the document, grabbed his envelope without so much as looking at it, and went back into the dorm. He walked in the entrance and made his way upstairs to his cell. Flip was sitting on his bunk when he walked in.

"What they say, cuz?"

"Shit." J-Bo plopped down on the bottom bunk and held up the envelope. "One of them janky ass lawyers is writing us again. I don't know why the fuck Mr. Luis don't tell them to stop." He flicked the envelope to Flip and collapsed back onto his bed. Flip looked at the name of the sender.

"Oh shit! J-Bo!" Flip hollered, jumping from his bunk.

****

"Ain't no mothafuckin' way," Chingy said. He was distressed, tripping about the message he'd gotten from Ken last night. He was drilling himself about not checking the phone when he felt it vibrate.

"Don't sit here stressing yourself, baby." It was Pumpkin's attempting to comfort him. "What's done is done. You can't change it." Her head was in his lap, and he sat with his back against the headboard. The two had decided to get a cheap hotel room on Six Flags Drive after the execution. She wanted to stay in Atlanta, but Chingy wanted to fall all the way back on some just in case type shit.

Until now, and to this degree, Pumpkin had never been in his business, but he'd needed one to talk to, so heavy was the situation. A week ago, Pumpkin was nothing but the squad's freak, and now she's Chingy's boo. He didn't give a damn anymore. The deal was sealed last night, and he promised to kill her if she ever performed any sexual favors for any of his partners again or if she spoke of Slick Nick to anyone.

He looked down at her pretty brown face and balled his fist. "I guess you right, but damn, Ken."

She wrapped her soft hand over his boney fist. "Baby, you can't get mad at Ken. You should've just checked the message. Maybe you should call him and let him know how you feel.

Yeah, he thought. *Maybe I should.*

****

After his brief meeting with Susie, Ken took a shower in his bathroom, changed clothes in his walk-in closet, and sat back at his desk.

The paper Susie had presented to him was still there. He took it up and read it several times over before looking down at the name scribbled in blue ink.

Michael Rogers, Ken thought. *Who are you? Kill me and my homeboys?* Ken smiled and shook his head at the thought of somebody wanting to start beef with YoungBoss.

"Mr. Griffith." It was Khloe coming through over the intercom. "Nae Waters is on line one."

Ken pressed one and picked up the receiver. "What's up, babe?"

"Can I see you? Like now," she asked urgently.

"Sure, are you aiight?"

"Just come by the shop."

"Okay, gimmie a sec. I'm on the way." He hung up.

He was just about to call Chingy, but his phone rang, and it was Chingy calling him. Ken didn't want to hear that his message had arrived too late, but seeing that it did, he told Chingy to just lay low and not to worry about anything. He never mentioned that he didn't want to do it, and Ken never gave a reason as to why he changed his mind on the hit.

****

"Dear, Mr. Dew," Flip read aloud, sounding like a talk show host. "The requested test results are in. "You are 99.9% the father of Jerome Dew Jr." He glanced up to J-Bo before continuing. "The next pages are the actual tests and an explanation of how we line up the two blood samples-"

J-Bo held his hand up to halt Flip's reading. He didn't want to hear anymore. He smiled hard as thoughts of fun times he would have with his son came to his mind.

"Go call and check on my nephew, nigga." Flip laid the test on J-Bo's bed.

J-Bo leaped out of bed and ran to the phone. He dialed Shaneeka's number and listened to the teleprompter notify her that she had a pre-paid call from an inmate at the Fulton County Jail. On the other end, Shakeena was so excited to be hearing from him that she almost pressed the wrong button.

"Hello?"

Her shallow voice made him smile. "I got the test results."

****

The sun was out, and so was Ken. He was cruising down the street in his white Range Rover, zoned out, listening to Yo Gotti's *Art Of The Hustle.*

The salon was up ahead on the right. He was curious to know what was behind Nae's sense over the phone. He went over multiple scenarios, but his mind kept coming back to Diamond.

I know this lil hardheaded bitch better not have told Nae about our conversation. I told this bitch to keep it between us, he thought, turning into the salon's parking lot.

He parked next to Nae's silver Infiniti and checked himself in the mirror before he got out of the vehicle. He hit the key fob and locked his door, pausing to give his surroundings a once over. He had the strangest feeling all of a sudden that he was being watched. Noticing nothing out of the ordinary, he made his way inside. There was some commotion to his left, and he looked to see a group of young niggas running out of Family Dollar, laughing with snacks and drinks. They ran across the parking lot, and a Korean man came out of the store wagging his fist and yelling obscenities that he didn't understand. Ken smiled at the thought of his younger years as he opened the door and walked into the salon. Tisha and Angela were busy with clients when he entered, and there were three more women seated gossiping while they waited to get serviced.

"Where's Nae?" he asked whoever cared to answer.

Tisha pointed to the back and he went where directed—crossing the first threshold, another door ahead of him and one to either side. He peeped behind the door to the left: it was a bathroom. He opened the door directly ahead, and there she sat on one of the thrift store looking-ass sofas. The room was a small area with a thirty-inch flat screen television mounted on the eggshell-painted walls.

"Hey, baby. What's up?"

She didn't hear him come in and was startled by his presence. She jumped up and rushed into his arms with red-rimmed eyes. It was clear the problem wasn't about his call to Diamond. If not that, then what? He held her, afraid to ask. Then inevitably, "Baby, what's wrong?"

"They think I killed Nicholas." She pointed to the flat screen where a brown skin news anchorwoman with long black hair reported live from a crime scene in a Krispy Kreme parking lot. Behind her was yellow crime scene tape and what looked like a traffic stop. Atlanta Police and forensics were everywhere. It was apparent that a full-scale investigation was being conducted. Ken listened to the entire story, but the only part he gave a fuck about was the fact that "Police have no suspects at this time."

"Wait, what?" he grinned. "Who thinks you killed him?"

"The police; they came here today questioning me about where I was last night."

"Nae, please calm down, baby. You were with me all last night. They know damn well you ain't killed anybody. It's just protocol."

She pulled back and looked at him. "But-"

Ken pulled her back in and held her. "It's just protocol."

****

After storming out of the house, Mike went to the address provided by Google and lurked around the area where he eventually saw someone that matched Ken's description exiting the building and hopping into a white Range Rover. Mike carefully followed him all the way to the south side to where he now waited across the street from the place Ken made his first stop: Universal Salon & Supplies. He sat behind the wheel, clutching his nine, thinking hard about running in and killing Ken.

So that's you, huh? Mike thought. *Big, office work doin' ass nigga.* He was tempted to run straight off in that bitch now and spray everybody while the nigga was getting his hair done.

****

A knock at the door brought Diamond awake. "Come in!" she called, lifting the cover away from her head, turning as Garrett walked through the door.

"Oh my god, Garrett!" She jumped from the bed and into his arms, wrapping her legs around his waist. He gripped her tight, and she felt the love. At that moment, she knew he had been missing her, just as she had been missing him.

He loosened his grip and put her down. "Baby, I don't think this shit is safe."

"What's not safe?"

"This whole testifying thing. I mean, it can get you killed, bae." He took a seat on the small sofa, and she sat on his lap.

"I know, bae, but-" She sucked her teeth, knowing he wouldn't understand her disposition.

"But nothing, Diamond. I came here because that case is all over the news, and it says their trial will start soon. I really love you, baby, and would hate to see something happen to you."

She already had her mind made up; she didn't give a damn what Garrett or anyone else said. She would not renege on delivering justice to that poor family. "Baby, if I cop out now, I'll go to jail."

"Yea, like they did me. Now I'm on six months' probation."

"Oh my god, baby. You were in jail?" She rubbed his face.

"Yes, but that's not the point."

She started to grind on him, hoping he would leave the subject alone and be ready to fuck. He pushed her to the floor and stood up. "What's wrong wit'chu, shawty? Why can't you see what I see? Let me tell you what's gone happen." He stood over her with his finger in her face. "You gone go in that courtroom, getting all in them folks' business, and they gon' send somebody to kill you. Baby, please don't put me through that. I don't know what I'll do without you."

She dropped her head. "Garrett, you know I love you with all my heart." She looked back up into his eyes. "But I'm the only one that can give justice to those families."

"And when you dead, who tha fuck gonna come forward and give me and Nae some justice?" His eyes watered. "Huh!?"

She stood and gripped his arm. "Baby, nobody is gonna kill me."

Garrett already knew the game. He was a real street nigga born and raised in the trenches of Atlanta; he just decided to go straight after seeing so much snake shit happen.

"Diamond," he took a deep breath. "Two teenagers were killed. The girl was pregnant. Do you really think they would mind killing you? A grown-ass woman? Of course not."

"Bae, they are in jail. That's why I'm doing this to put them away. They can't hurt me from there."

"Diamond, when you're a killer, you hang with other killers. Your name is in their paperwork, don't you know that? Don't you know you're in a fucking protection program for a reason?"

"I don't care, Garrett. I'm testifying."

Garrett stared into Diamond's eyes, and in them, he could see that he had lost this one. No matter what he said, no matter what he did, she was testifying. He pulled his arms back from her.

"I love you." He kissed her forehead and walked out the door.

****

"Excuse me real quick, baby." He broke their embrace to answer his phone without even looking at the name of the caller.

"Hello?" He listened for a few seconds before looking back at his Rolex. "Gotdammit, Mr. Luis, I apologize. It totally slipped my mind. No, I'm not that far. Give me a few." He hung up and pulled Nae back into his embrace. "Baby, I'm sorry, but I have to go. I forgot I have to meet this damn lawyer today."

"What for?"

"He has to explain some flaws he found in a few contracts for me."

Nae released a heavy sigh. "Ok, but baby, the way that detective was looking and questioning me, it kinda bothers me still."

"Did you kill him?" Ken smirked.

"Hell no!"

He chuckled. "Well, you have nothing to worry about."

****

J-Bo had been given his lawyer Ken's contact info so they could link up and devise a good plan, but he never used it until the other day, and they scheduled a time and place to meet.

As Ken turned out the parking lot of the salon, he noticed the black Equinox across the street come alive. The vehicle turned out. It was odd because he didn't see anyone enter the vehicle, which means they had to have been lurking there. After a few minutes of driving, he looked in his rearview mirror, and the black Equinox was behind him. Just to ensure he wasn't tripping, he quickly quirked into the left lane without a turning signal. The light had just turned red, and he was now side by side with the Equinox. He rolled his window down, ready to check the driver.

****

"Man, what do you want?" Mike answered his phone.

"Michael, where are you? Don't do nothing stupid?" Pops spat.

"Man, I'm posted up right now, waiting on this nigga. I done followed him. He in a fucking beauty supply or some shit. I guess he gettin' his hair done. I'm finna kill dis nigga, Pops!"

"Michael, what the fuck did I tell yo stupid fuckin ass-"

Mike ended the call when Ken came from the salon. The man's return was quick, and Mike's mind was racing with options. Should he pull up over there and smoke the nigga before he got in his Rover, or should he wait for a better opportunity?

Ken was moving kind of quick, clearly in a rush to get where he was headed next.

Wherever that may be, Mike thought, *you not finna make it there.*

Mike started his engine and turned out a car behind Ken. He drove with his left hand with the Pistol in his right. All of a sudden, Ken quickly shot into the left lane. The light turned red, and their vehicles were adjacent to one another, Ken on his left. Mike's heart rate accelerated. His palms sweated. He slid his 9mm to his left hand and gripped the wheel with his right.

Just roll down and dump, Mike told himself. He looked around to ensure there was nothing flakey or no one along with Ken. Everything seemed normal. The light turned green, and just as he was about to execute the move, an Atlanta City Police cruiser turned from the far end of the street onto the road. He quickly dropped his weapon and hit the gas. Seething, he slammed his fist on the steering wheel. "Fuck!"

****

Ken stood at the front of the Peachtree restaurant and peered around in an attempt to try his eye at spotting a crooked lawyer. He approached the table of a chunky, forty-year-old-looking man. He figured he was at the right table because J-Bo had already told him the man was Jewish, and he sported a necklace with a six-point star emblem.

"Mr. Luis?" he asked.

"That's me." He stood and greeted Ken with a handshake. "Tell me something I don't know, Mr. Ken." They took their seats, and Mr. Luis sipped his tea. There was thick smoke coming from the cup.

"I spoke to the witness and offered her fifty grand not to testify." Mr. Luis raised his eyebrows hopefully.

Ken sighed. "She declined."

"Speak to her again, double the money." He sipped his cup again.

"I wish it was that easy, but she's saying it's not about the money. She wants to give justice to society and their families."

Mr. Luis scoffed. He looked down and around the establishment before turning back to Ken. "This little cock-sucking-bitch is a pain in my fucking ass," he said through clenched teeth. His kid-like voice sounded more mature this time.

"Yea, mines too."

"Mr. Ken, please listen to me very, very closely." He stood and grabbed his jacket from the back of the chair. Digging through his pocket, he dropped a ten-dollar bill on the table.

The pale face waiter approached. The boy was bone-rail thin and reminded Ken of those Vampires in *Twilight*. He grabbed the bill. "I'll get your change, sir."

Mr. Luis fanned him off. "Don't bother. Keep it."

"Oh, thank you. You're done with this?" He reached for his cup. He nodded and motioned for Ken to stand up.

He stood, and Mr. Luis embraced him in a handshake-hug and whispered in his ear. "If you ever want to see your brother on this side of the world again, this is what needs to happen, no exceptions. Speak to her again; double the money. If she turns it down this time, she must die. Make it quick and quiet."

CHAPTER 11

"Ion trust these bitches, and Ion't fuck wit these niggas, got fifty grand in my britches on my waistline is dat fifty, ayo ayooo!" Lil Dread yelled into the mic as he ran around the stage. He was turnt in that bitch. It had gotten so hot; he took off his shirt, and the crowd went mayhem when he threw it to them. He was accompanied by twenty other men. They all wore either hoodies or t-shirts with YBE printed on the front and back in black or blue letters. The guys with the black letters wore royal blue hoodies, and the guys with the royal blue letters wore black shirts. Fifteen of the men on stage were turning up with Lil Dread. The other five were standing still and observing their surroundings. Those were the niggas that were strapped. The crowd jumped up and down, bopping their heads, as they sang along. "Ayo ayooooo!"

Ken was in the VIP section above the stage nursing a red plastic cup of Cîroc as he looked down at the hyped club through his Louis V. shades. He really didn't feel like being there, but he wanted to support Lil Dread. The DJ shouted him and his team out and raised his cup high in salute.

"Dread doin' his thang," Chingy said at Ken's side. "Dis music shit gon' get big."

There were twenty people in their private section. Only eight of them belonged to YoungBoss, and the other twelve were exotic strippers. The money was flowing, and they were showing out.

"Yea, he is." Ken sipped his drink. "He deserves these thirty." The club was actually paying fifty grand for the performance, but he kept twenty for himself.

"Aye, big bruh." Chingy elbowed him, staring deeply into the crowd.

“What?” Ken followed Chingy’s stare but saw nothing out of the ordinary.

“Dis nigga been lookin’ up here every two minutes.”

“Who?” Ken still didn’t see.

“Da nigga at the bar wearing all da grey, look.” Chingy nodded inconspicuously toward the bar. He was staring at the stage, playing it smooth.

Knowing how Chingy could be on some extra paranoid shit, Ken decided to put it to the test. He turned his head almost all the way towards the stage to appear as if he was focused on Lil Dreads performance while surreptitiously cutting his eyes towards the man at the bar. To his surprise, Chingy wasn’t tripping. The nigga was definitely hawking.

****

“Girl, you is stupid!” Nae laughed with Tisha as they cleaned the salon.

“I’m for real, girl. He gotta work for this pussy.” She stood like a model, resting her left hand on her meaty hip and using her right hand to point at her crotch.

Tisha stood 6’1”. Some considered her big-boned, some considered her just right, while others felt as if she was two cheeseburgers away from being fat. “So, if he comes in late with a bullshit excuse, no pussy for a week!”

They both laughed. Nae swept up all the hair, and Tisha was working on placing all the supplies back to where they were supposed to go.

“I can’t believe how busy it’s been today,” Nae said. Acknowledging the fact business hadn’t been this good for some time.

“Yea, maybe you should hire some more bitches,” Tisha said.

After her attack, Nae had fired everybody except for Angela, feeling some kind of way about nobody calling the police for her. Plus, Angela had always come correct with her weekly pay without Nae having to push up. The other bitches did the exact opposite. It's a wonder she hadn't fired them all before the incident.

Nae counted through the day's earnings, gave Tisha her cut, and took the rest to her safe in the back. Tisha was finished, purse in hand, and ready to go when Nae returned.

"Girl, I'm about to go to Ken's house and take me a long, hot bubble bath," Nae said, keying in the numeric password to the security system. They stepped outside and were blinded by white and blue flashing. There were two crown Vic's, and an officer jumped out of each vehicle wearing an APD jacket with their weapons drawn. Two other officers remained seated in squad cars.

"Freeze!" An officer shouted. "Put ya hands where I can see them!"

"For what?" Nae yelled back. "We didn't do anything!"

Once he was close enough, he gave Nae a forceful blow to the stomach. She squawked, dropping to her hands and knees.

"Why the fuck did you hit her, mothafucka? She just got out the fuckin' hospital!"

"Shut the fuck up," the second officer said. He grabbed Tisha by the back of her neck, mushed her into the store's glass window, and cuffed her aggressively as she resisted arrest. "Stop resisting!"

"What the fuck is fuck is going on?" Tisha continued to struggle, defiantly. "You aren't telling us anything?"

I said stop!" The officer punched her in the kidney, grabbed the back of her head, and slammed her face into the window. "Fuckin' resisting!"

Tisha began to fall but was caught and held up by the officer while he finished cuffing her. She couldn't breathe. All the wind had left her body.

Nae was snatched to her feet, cuffed, and presented with no rights. They were put roughly in the back of each unmarked car.

****

"Give me a martini" Ferrari told the bartender. She took a quick glance at Mike. He looked at Ken's section once more, then a wicked grin covered his face. When her drink was ready, she got it and walked away. Ferrari was a beautiful, redboned dancer. Every nigga that visited the club wanted to fuck her on sight and for the right price, they could. She had a twenty-inch waist with a big onion booty. She wore a skimpy pink bra and a matching thong that was buried in her ass cheeks. She and Mike were high school sweethearts. After a few years, unfortunately, they realized they weren't compatible, and they broke up to remain close friends and fuck partners. She was down with the plan to set up Ken because Jon was like a little brother to her and her love for Mike still ran deeper than an ocean.

Three strippers entered YBE's section with a complimentary bottle of Ace of Spades on the house. They hooped and hollered in celebration as the DJ constantly shouted out YoungBoss.

"Hey, I'm Ferrari." She approached; her hand stretched.

Ken nodded. "I'm Ken." He shook her hand.

"Like I didn't know that," she joked.

He cracked a smile, and Chingy sat idly by as they chopped it up for a while. Chingy didn't like the smell of the girl, feeling she had some ties to the guy at the bar. He looked down, but the man was gone. Chingy made several unsuccessful attempts at getting Ken to acknowledge that the girl wasn't right, but Ken was lost in a trance, all touchy-feely. Frustrated at his failed attempts, Chingy decided to let it be and leave him with the girl.

"You ready to go?" Ken asked Ferrari. "You got me horny as fuck."

"I can tell." She smiled, gripping his hardened dick through his pants. She stood up.

"Y'all niggas hold Dread down," Ken told his team before leaving.

Mike had changed seats, getting closer to the door. With Ken taking the bait, he ran to his car.

****

Chingy sat behind the wheel of his car, furious that Ken was going for whatever bullshit that stripper was saying to him. Ken was a vet in his eyes, and he felt as if he should have known better than that.

The man in gray came jogging out, and Chingy was even more furious. Who the fuck was this nigga, and what the fuck was he trying? Chingy wanted so bad to jump out and kill the nigga, but he hadn't been given the green light to do so.

****

Ferrari was lying her ass off, telling Ken that she did real estate in New York and was currently in school for physical therapy.

She paused her storytelling to send a text.

"No texting in my ride, baby," Ken said.

Having dealt with enough rappers and important people to know their state of mind, she dropped the phone in her purse without even finishing the message.

Using his free hand, he moved the light fabric from over her pussy and massaged her clit. She squeezed his arm and moaned softly. He fingered her, and she bit down on her lip. She looked in the rearview before grabbing his dick again through his pants.

"I want some head," Ken said.

She smiled, tightening her grip on him. "I got you as soon as we get to the room, big man."

A chrome .45 was suddenly in his hand, held against the side of her head.

"No, bitch. You gonna do it right now." She didn't hesitate to pull out his manhood and suck it like a Popsicle on a hot summer day. "And you bet not stop either. Ugh, shit, you better not stop bitch." He groaned, pressing the barrel firmly to her back, a continuous reminder of its presence. Ken rode around the city in bliss, making random turns as Ferrari sucked for her life. Feeling as though her well-being depended on it, she gave the wettest, nastiest, sloppiest head she ever had. Before long, Ken was rising up in his seat, feeling the sensation build.

"Ugghh, fuck! Mmmmm." He released in her mouth, and she swallowed without having to be told.

Then, at forty-five miles per hour, he suddenly slammed on the brakes, nearly causing a three-car collision. His tires made a loud screech as the Range Rover came to a full stop. Ken pointed the weapon at Ferrari's head.

The man in all-gray, trailing behind Ken in an Equinox, saw clear what took place, understanding that his cover was blown. He swerved left to avoid a collision, cut back, and made a sharp right at the light, barely missing a tan Buick Century. The driver of which blared the horn furiously.

Chingy was behind the Equinox. He swerved into the left lane, ready to pursue, but Ken honked twice, calling him off.

"Get the fuck out my shit, bitch! And tell that nigga-" He pointed his pistol in the direction the Equinox had fled, then to her head again. "Matter fact, who the fuck is that nigga, anyway, huh?"

"I don't know," she cried, "I swear to God!" She held her hand up protectively as if the gesture could stop bullets.

"You don't know!?"

"He just paid me to ride with you. I don't know him from a can of paint. I swear to God!"

He sucked his teeth. "Get the fuck out!"

"Give me this shit, hoe!" He ripped and snatched her clothes off before kicking her out in the middle of the street.

CHAPTER 12

"I'm sorry that shit happened to you like that, shawty," Mike said to Ferrari. They were in Ferrari's bed, in a one-bedroom apartment in Dogwood Apartments on Bankhead. He had come back for her last night. The idea of Ken hurting her is what made him bust a U-turn and return to the scene, clutching his gun, ready for whatever. It broke his heart to see her butt naked and walking the streets like that, crying and shaking.

She relayed the events, and he wasn't convinced the man had peeped game, but was certain the fault was her own. The fact he sympathized with what she'd gone through is why he didn't snap on her.

"I'ma off that nigga," Mike swore. "On my mama!"

"Baby," she yawned. "Just leave that shit alone." "That nigga smart. Just catch him slippin' whenever you can." She stretched out, remembering how scared she was the night before.

"Nah, fuck all dat shit." He pushed her away and stood. He was clothed in only boxers. "Dem hoe ass niggas killed my brotha and sista." He paced the floor.

She got up and strutted towards him in the nude. "Michael, you and I both know that the niggas that did that shit are in jail." She eyed him, trying to make sense of the whole situation.

He continued to pace, purposely breaking eye contact. "Yea," he huffed. "But this nigga is the closest one to dem niggas in jail, so he gotta go."

She grabbed his arm. He snatched away.

"And what is killing them gonna do, Mike? It ain't gon' bring Jon and Rika back."

His cell phone rang. It was Pops. He'd been ignoring the calls all night because he felt like his father was on some scary shit and all he wanted to do was give a speech. Now, he was irritated with Ferrari, and he decided to hear what his father had to say.

"Aye, shawty, my pops been blowin' me up all night. I'm finna slide through and see what's up."

He dressed in his black and white Adidas jogger, slipped his feet into his Adidas house shoes, gargled some mouth-wash, kissed her cheek, and left.

****

Angela pulled into the salon's parking lot and gobbled down the remains of her cream cheese bagel before she parked. She noticed Nae's car and smiled. Her girl had come far from their days in the hood, doing hair out of an apartment once lived in together. Their dream of owning their own salon had been long in coming. Nae had been the first to succeed, and she'd hired Angela on, promising to help her get her own salon one day. She always talked to her about the legal side, the building code, and licensing required to make it official. It seems overwhelming sometimes, but Angela felt she could manage.

She fished through her purse to find the loose key before she got out of her Kia, headed for the salon. A set of keys were on the ground, just outside the salon's door. She recognized the pink covering around one of the keys, and she knew they belonged to Nae.

Angela frowned as she bent to pick them up, exposing the top part of her wrinkled butt crack. The salon's lights were off, but the door was unlocked. Was the girl inside? If so, why were the main lights off? And why were the keys on this side of the door? Something wasn't quite right. She looked to Nae's car in the parking lot before she opened the salon's door- startled by the alarm. Heart racing, Angela hurried to deactivate the system.

Something definitely wasn't right, she thought, moving cautiously around the shop in search of anything out of place. With no sign of Nae, she took up her phone and dialed her friend's number several times with no answer. She tried Tisha's phone and got the same results.

The arrival of the first customer shifted her thoughts from concerned to business. Nae was bound to show and provide the answer to all her questions.

****

Pops was sitting on the couch grinning when his son entered the front door.

"What the hell you in here smirkin' about scary ass nigga?"

"Have a seat," Pops directed.

He complied, curious now.

Pops stood. "My young and dumb son. When I say chill out and let me handle shit, that's exactly what I mean. I'm yo father; not the otha way around."

Mike knew something was up, but he couldn't say what.

"It's that way for a reason, son. I have a lot more of this." He tapped his temple.

Mike sucked his teeth. "Man, get to da point, old-ass nigga."

Pops chuckled. "Don't make me get on yo lil fat head ass. Now follow me." He walked towards one of the back rooms, and Mike reluctantly followed.

****

Ken yawned into the phone, listening to the jail's recording. He pressed five when prompted. "What's up, J-Bo?"

"Same shit, shawty. Aye, set up a visit, gotta holla at you."

"I already got one for tomorrow. I'm gonna holla at the bitch again today, man. Hopefully, things go better this time."

"Bet, what about that hoe, Nae?"

Hearing her name being disrespected like that, especially knowing there was nothing he could do about it, drove him crazy.

"Everything is good, bro. She's doing just what I need her to do."

"Aiight, shawty, I was just checkin' in." He hung up.

Ken stretched out really good, cracking his bones, and yawned a few more times before checking his phone. He had no missed calls from the queen bee. He had that one text from her where she was telling him she was about to leave the salon and go to his house. He'd given her a key the day they made love for the first time.

She'd wanted him to call after the club. *No matter how late,* her text read. *Talk to me 'til you get here.*

After his incident with Ferrari, he called four times with no answer. He figured she'd fallen asleep, but with her absent when he arrived, he called twice more with no answer still.

Ken got up to brush his teeth. He was tempted to call Nae, but he'd been doing so with no results since last night, and he didn't want to come off as desperate, or worse, possessive. Instead, after brushing his teeth, he called Diamond. When she didn't answer, he sent a text to let her know it was him. She called right after she read the text.

"Those people," he told her, "have added the value of $50k to their original offer. That's $100k in cash, Diamond".

She refused, and he elaborated his opinion of the danger her life could be in by going through with this, careful not to sound threatening nor involved, but concerned and caring instead. She told him she would consider the offer and get back with him.

He reminded her not to mention the conversation to Nae. This time, however, there was something to the way he said it. Her hand began to shake. She felt like it was now or never to tell Nae about her feelings for Ken and their private conversations.

She hung up with Ken and called Nae ten times back-to-back and got the voicemail each time.

****

"Wala!" Pops said, swinging open the bedroom door open and flipping on the light. There were two women on the bed, naked, handcuffed, blindfolded, and gagged with dirty socks. A shoestring was used to hold the cloth in place.

The sight of them squirming and kicking along with their muffled exclamations was comical to Mike. He turned his nose at the smell of dry urine. What kind of kinky shit was Pops on? This was something of the man he hadn't known. If Pops expected him to participate in… whatever the hell it was he had going on, he had to be out of his fucking mind!

Pops removed the blindfold from the women's face. Both of their eyes were puffy from crying, and the light skin girl's face was red. They looked around the small furniture less room, seeing the boarded windows along with the fact their captors wore no masks, their hearts sank; they were going to die.

"My young and dumb son," Pops said, looking from Mike to one of the ladies. "This is Nae Waters. And this is um..." He snatched the shoestring from the other girl's face. Her gag reflex forced her to spit the cloth out. "What's ya name, sweetie?"

"Wh- who are you?" she stammered. "Where are we?"

Pops slapped the chunky bitch across the face. "Bitch, I asked for ya name!"

"Tisha!" she cried.

"And this is Ms. Tisha," he made the introductions.

Irritated, Mike shrugged his shoulders. "Yeah, yeah. But who the fuck are these bitches?"

"Well, Nae and Tisha are friends, I guess." He looked at Tisha for clarification, and she nodded. "But, Ms. Nae," Pops rubbed her face. "Is the girlfriend of our good friend Mr. Kenneth."

Mike's eyes grew wide. "How da fuck you-"

"I told you to let me make some calls, lil young and dumb ass nigga." He crossed his arms. "I'm the mothafuckin' dun dotta." He was acting like the streets just laid the information down in his hands, but he would never tell his son the truth, that he'd hired an expensive private investigator to follow Ken, having told the investigator he and Ken were in a relationship, and he suspected Ken of having an affair with a woman. The PI soon gave him several photos of Ken and Nae together on several different occasions. He soon dismissed the PI and tried to pursue Ken on his own. He couldn't keep up, however; Ken was too smooth and unpredictable. Also, Ken drove through certain hoods, into which Pops couldn't follow at the risk of being stopped, check, and likely killed.

With that, he decided Nae was easier prey with her set schedule for the salon. That being the case, Pops had some of his dogs assist him with the kidnap, posing as cops so they would be able to avoid unnecessary incidents.

CHAPTER 13

Diamond had recently spoken to Mr. Anderson, ensuring him that she was more than ready to serve justice to the families of those two victims. Afterwards, she called Nae, as she had many times before, and got no answer. She sent several texts and called again with the same results.

"Nae, baby, come on," Diamond whined.

It wasn't like her sister to not answer her call or to not respond in any manner whatsoever. She thought of Ken and the possibility of him having done something to Nae.

She didn't want to speak to him, but she needed to check on her sister, and if anyone knew her whereabouts, it was him. With that, she reluctantly dialed his number.

"Hey, Ken. It's Diamond." She thought of how to check him without really checking him.

"I'm glad you called," he said. "I believe you're making a great decision."

"Um, Ken," she hesitated, trying to find the right words to break it to him. "That's not why I'm calling."

"It isn't?" His disappointment was clear with just those words.

"No. I'm trying to get in touch with Nae. I haven't talked to her all day; I figured she would be with you."

"I haven't spoken with her either," he said.

They were both quiet.

"If she doesn't hit me back soon," Ken said. "I'll go by the shop. I'm sure it's nothing major, though."

"Ok, Just let me know something because this isn't like her."

"Ok and... Diamond." He hoped she hadn't hung up yet.

"Yes?"

"What about the other situation we spoke of?"

Diamond was suddenly terrified, convinced Ken had something to do with Nae's mysterious whereabouts. It was rather implicit, the way he came back to the subject. It seemed to suggest she comply. What would become of her sister if she didn't? How would justice be served if she did? She wasn't sure, but Nae was more important.

She sighed. "Ok, I'll do it. Now, who do I talk to about my money?"

"I'll make the appropriate call to get your money today. Just be on standby for my call." Ken could barely contain his excitement

His boy was coming home.

****

"I swear to God, I don't know anything about what he does," Nae said. "All I know is he runs a music group or something like that, and I really don't even know much about that." She took a few deep breaths. The three-hour interrogation had gone nowhere.

In a plastic lawn chair across from the bed, Mike sat smoking a cigarette.

"Can you turn on a fan or something?" Tisha asked, coughing from the thick smoke.

Ignoring her request, Mike passed the cigarette to Pops, who sat on the foot of the bed. He took a long drag from the cigarette and flicked the ashes on Tisha's naked body. "Girl," he said emotionlessly, "shet tha fuck up."

"So, you have no idea why I would wanna get at him?" Mike asked.

Nae shook her head.

"Bitch, you know dem niggas killed my folks! Stop lying."

Nae, through all her distress, wondered what Ken had gotten her into.

Pops shifted to Nae's side of the bed. "I'ma make this really easy for you, Lil mama. Whether you know about it or not." He inhaled and passed the short to Mike. "I don't give a fuck. I want him, not you."

"Man, let us the fuck go!" Tisha cried. "Somebody help us, please!"

Pops was quick to deliver a series of slaps to Tisha's face. "Now, didn't I say shet tha fuck up?"

****

"Good morning, Mr. Crane." Angela greeted, entering the dollar store that was in the same plaza as Nae's salon. Mr. Crane was an old Korean man that bought into the Family Dollar franchise. He was standing behind the desk filing his nails when she entered.

"Ms. Angela." He waved.

He was familiar with the girls by their first names from their frequent visits to his store for snacks and small hair accessories in case they ran out and needed something really quick.

Walking back towards the register, she had two twenty-ounce Sprites, two; family-sized bags of spicy nacho Doritos, and a box of zebra cakes. He knew for a fact all of that was for her personally. He discreetly shook his head at her walking with the snacks, thinking how disgusting she looked. Mr. Crane couldn't stand a woman that was big and sloppy like her. Something was different about her that morning. A weird silence, she would usually be in there talking his ears off, trying to flirt and shit.

"How are you feeling today?" he faked a smile.

"I'm ok, hun, just a rough start."

I wonder what's the matter with sasquatch, he thought.

"It will get better." He began to ring up her items. "How is Miss Nae"? He accepted the ten-dollar bill she'd just handed him.

"Um, fine, I guess. I hadn't talked to her today."

"She's a big girl. She'll be okay."

She searched his face for answers from that comment, but his blank expression told nothing. The door swung open.

"Angela, don't forget, I gotta be to work in an hour." Her impatient client came over to give her a frustrating reminder.

"I'm coming now, girl."

"Looks like somebody is busy today." He handed her the change and bagged her items.

"Yea, I will come back and talk to you before I go home; let me get back over there." She turned to leave.

"Hey, I will help with her bond money if that's the problem, as long as I am reimbursed."

She turned around and frowned, thinking shortly before speaking to make sure she wasn't hearing shit. "What are you talking about, Mr. Crane?"

"Miss Nae and the new girl, they were arrested last night."

He pointed to the parking lot; her silence let him know that this was her first time hearing it. "Police brutality, too. One of them punched Miss Nae in the stomach, and another slam new girl head into store window. I saw the whole thing, but me no know who to call. Usually, the police, but if they are the ones committing the crimes then…" He threw his arms up in surrender.

Nae's car is still there. The door is unlocked. Her keys are on the ground.

It all made sense now.

"Oh my god, do you know why?"

"Not sure. I only know what I told you. Did you hear what I say about your friends?"

"Yes." Angela had definitely heard what he said about the police brutality, but she was more concerned about what they had been arrested for leaving out the shop in the first place.

"I hope they catch the kids who keep stealing from my store and do them like that. Always come, and no buy."

****

Tez had just kicked Pumpkin in the face, knocking her unconscious as Ken walked through the door. He paused, unhappy with what he'd run into.

"What the fuck is this?" he said.

"Peanut," Tez called through the open door to one of the two YBE affiliates on the porch. "Get this hoe out of here." To Ken, he said, "She ain't dead homie."

"Where the fuck is Chingy?" he growled, disappointed that he was letting shit like go down in their place of business.

Tez pointed towards the back and followed after Ken, leaving Peanut to deal with Pumpkin.

Chingy was standing at the dining room table, feeding money in the machine with one hand, using his shirt for nursing his bleeding eye with his other hand.

"The fuck going on in here, man?" Ken asked.

"Nun major," Chingy said.

"I'ma have to go through this shit with you later," Ken said. "I don't have time right now." He began stuffing the counted money in a small brown bag. "How much is this?"

"Sixty," Chingy said, wiping his eye.

"Man, go clean that shit up," Ken ordered. He gestured at Tez. "Come help me count this money, lil bra."

Tez approached the table. "How much?"

"Sixty more," Ken said. "And what the hell happened?"

"To make a long story short, she says he da daddy, and he snapped."

Ken frowned. Tez laughed hard.

At last, Ken said, "I know he didn't go out like that, right?"

Tez shrugged his shoulders.

Once the money was proper, they added it to the small bag, and Ken headed out.

Peanut was on the porch, and there was no sign of Pumpkin.

"Everything cool, lil bra?"

"Yea, when that hoe woke up trippin', I gave her $200 to just leave."

Ken smiled, liking how young Peanut thought. He dug in his pocket and peeled off $500 for him.

"Keep thinking that way, and you'll go far."

****

Having climbed from the third-story balcony, working her precarious way down to the next one below, Diamond prayed that she didn't regret her decision. She wanted only the safety of her sister; certain she was in jeopardy. With her father away and her mother gone, Nae was all she had left. She couldn't recall a single moment since the death of their mother where she couldn't reach her sister or that a missed call wasn't immediately returned. But now, with the appearance of her new boyfriend, she's unavailable all of a sudden. And with his stupid proposition not to testify, it made it hard to see it anyway but the way she saw it currently: Ken was in some way involved. True enough, she wanted justice for the family of the ones murdered, but not at her sister's expense. Again, she wasn't sure, but could she risk it being otherwise?

She considered Slick Nick's death and felt Ken had something to do with that as well, though she had no more proof of that than she did of with her belief that he was behind Nae's disappearance.

Now, climbing across the rail of the second-floor balcony, Diamond lowered herself to the furthest extent, swinging some fifteen feet above the ground. She didn't want to let go, but neither time nor gravity would permit her to hang long. She would rather let go and drop than lose her grip and drop still. With that, she braced herself and let go.

"Oooh!" she cried on impact. Her leg gave way, and her butt kissed the ground. She sat nursing her ankle, but only for a second.

"Oh, dear," someone said. It was an elderly white woman leaving her car. "Are you okay?"

"I'm fine," Diamond said, coming to her feet. She felt anything but fine. However, her ankle felt broke. Even so, she half ran, half hobbled across the grassy area that separated the hotel from a raggedy carwash where Ken waited in his white Range Rover.

****

"Hey, baby, it's me," Ken said to Nae's voicemail. "Just wondering why I haven't heard from you." He thought of what more to say but concluded with, "Hit me back."

He hung up just as Diamond came limping his way.

"Ahh, fuck!" she moaned, sliding into the passenger seat, closing the door, and massaging her left ankle. She took off her shoe.

"You aiight?" Ken said.

"Feels like my whole leg is broken."

He examined her leg; her foot was red and swollen. "What happened?"

She rolled her neck. "I just jumped out of that high ass window. That's what happened!"

"You'll be aiight." He merged into traffic.

"I think I broke my ankle. You talked to, Nae?"

"I doubt it. It's probably sprained and not yet. I just left a message. I'm sure she will call me back sometime soon."

He didn't seem the least bit concerned. "So, what's up with my money?"

He nodded towards the back. A brown paper bag sat on the seat. "I picked it up before we met." He looked at his phone, wishing for a call or text from Nae.

It wasn't long before Ken turned into a very cheap and rugged Cottage Inn. Two crackheads were on the curb, and Diamond screwed her face at the quality of the place. To say it didn't compare to the Sheraton Hotel was an understatement. She had gone from riches to roaches. Literally!

Ken read her reaction. "It's fine," he assured her. "You'll only be here for a few days."

"Okay," Nae countered. "And why couldn't I be somewhere nice for a few days?"

"Because all the nice hotels have top-notch surveillance. When they realize you're gone, they will do a statewide search. They will check everywhere, except for places like this."

It made sense, but she still wasn't happy about it. *You lucky I love you, Nae. Just come back to me safe.*

Ken parked in front of the last building and reached for the bag from the back. "One-hundred thousand." He dropped it on her lap. He removed an electronic key card from the glove compartment and handed it to her. "Room 202. Please don't leave until I let you know it's safe. Like I said, only a few days."

"Okay, what am I gonna eat, wear, do? How can I just stay put in this piece of shit?"

He gave a cold stare. "There's food in there. Plus, you have enough money to order food. There is a nice white robe in there, and you can wear that. I will let you know when I hear from Nae. Please get out now."

Diamond rolled her eyes but did as she was told. She entered the room and was suddenly even more aware of the change from her previous accommodations. The place was filthy, and she was near to walking back out before she even closed the door, but then she thought of Nae, of how her every question to Ken in regard to her hung on her reply to nonsense.

She forced aside her negative thoughts and the whereabouts of Nae. With that, she felt some type of way for not delivering the appropriate justice to the families of those teens. At the same time, there was a sense of relief from the pressure of having to do so.

Diamond tossed the money on the bed and crawled in beside it.

CHAPTER 14

Ken was so excited to relay the good news to J-Bo, he drove to the jail and spoke with the sheriff himself, requesting his tomorrow's visit's to be rescheduled for today. The sheriff laughed in his face, but reconsidered when Ken slid him five-thousand dollars and asked to have the visit arranged immediately.

"What's good, my boy?" he greeted J-Bo with a tight hug.

"Same shit, ready to come home." They sat. "I thought the visit wasn't till tomorrow."

"I'ma boss. I do what I want when I want."

They laughed. "Anyway."

"Anyway, y'all niggas gone be home real soon. Ima be outside in that white Lamb."

J-Bo smiled. Ken only brought his white Lamborghini Gallardo out for special occasions. "That bitch been parked for so long; you sure it still work?"

"Yea, my shit work, nigga. How y'all holding up?"

"We good, man."

"Okay, the bitch got the money, and I got her ducked off somewhere real low-key until the trial is over with."

"Damn, Ken, I owe you my life, bro," he exhaled deeply. "I love you, bro."

Ken fanned him off. He wasn't with all that emotional shit. "Man, this shit is child's play. Next time… Kill the witness." They both laughed.

"Make sure you hit the lawyer and let him know what's up," J-Bo said. "And what's up with Lil Dread's ugly ass? I saw him in the *Hip-Hop Weekly* magazine. That young nigga piped. Tell him I said keep it up."

"No doubt, I'm gonna hit the lawyer when I leave here. Man, Dread is doing his thing, man. I believe in the next four or five years, we gon' move up to a global status with this music shit. I'd seen a few pop artists I'm thinking about backing financially."

J-Bo smiled. "That's what's up. Everything else been straight, though?"

"Yea, somebody called my office the other day talking about he gone kill me and all my homeboys. I was thinking like, what the fuck," he explained the whole story.

"You got some uncooked beef out there?"

"With Chingy and Tez, it's all well done."

J-Bo nodded, knowing how reckless those two young niggas were. "You already done did ya homework?"

"Nah, man, my assistant traced the number. It came back as a..." He looked to the ceiling, trying to remember the name Susie had written down. "Rivers... Riley. . . Rogers. Yeah, that's it. Michael Rogers."

"Aye, you know the young nigga on my case, the last name is Rogers." He gravely thought they could be related.

"You know how many people got that name?"

"You're right, it's just hell of a coincidence. Just be on point, big bruh."

Ken nodded. They chatted a little more about their plans when the cousins were out until they were interrupted by the sheriff.

****

"Yea, mothafucka, yea!"

J-Bo leaped up the steps three at a time. County inmates from the phones, spades table and TV looked on, figuring his lawyer had just given him good news because he'd just came back from a visit, and it wasn't a regular visitation day.

"Who da hell dat was shawty?" Flip asked.

"We goin' home real soon, nigga." He punched Flip's arm.

"Oh, shit." He jumped from his bunk and started doing the shootout dance. He wanted to punch J-Bo back, but once he started playing, he was like one of those retarded kids that didn't understand the words quit. Stepping on the range, he announced, "Attention dorm, starting today, until me and J-Bo leave, we gone cook pockets, make cakes, and Bombay's fa the whole dorm! Y'all ain't gotta worry 'bout shit!"

The dorm erupted in claps, laughs, and cheers. They definitely had enough money to fulfill their promise, and everybody knew it. They went back into the cell, and J-Bo filled his cousin in on every word Ken had said.

****

On his way to Nae's salon, he found himself driving directly behind a black Equinox, the same model that had been tailing him recently. Ken's adrenaline kicked in. "C-O-V-I-9-6-4." he read the license plate number aloud before switching lanes, pulling alongside to peep the passenger side of the vehicle- relieved to find it was a woman behind the wheel.

In the salon's parking lot, Ken took a moment to call Mr. Luis and bring him up to date.

"Hello, Ken?" the man answered.

"The business is handled. We should be good soon, right?"

"Which route did you take?"

"PayPal."

"Alright, I'll be in touch soon. Please make sure your order is secure." Mr. Luis said before hanging up.

****

Entering the salon, Ken saw two girls sitting under hair dryers. Angela and another dark skin girl he hadn't seen before had clients in their chairs, while another sat waiting her turn, preoccupied with her phone.

The dark skin girl looked to Ken, but before she could speak, he asked, "Where's Nae?"

"Oh my God," Angela exclaimed. "You don't know? She hasn't called you yet? Nae's in jail, Ken."

He couldn't believe what he was hearing, and it took his mind a second to process the information. He couldn't imagine Nae doing anything to land her in jail. The incident with her and the homicide detective about Slick Nick's death was the first thing that came to mind. For her to be arrested on those charges said much for the detective's incompetence. Well, Ken had a lawyer for that. And when they were done suing the justice department, Nae would have a string of salons around the city.

"What the hell happened?" Ken wanted the details.

"I don't know," Angela shrugged. "Our neighbor," she pointed towards the dollar store. "Said Nae and Tisha went to jail last night, and he said the police officer punched Nae in the stomach."

"Tisha, too," the dark skin girl cut it. "Said they punched her and rammed her face into the window." She nodded her head to the front of the store.

Ken was taken back by the news, and it showed.

Angela went on to recall how she'd arrived this morning to find Nae's car in the lot, the keys on the ground, and the door unlocked.

"You called the police station?"

"No, I've been so busy, I hadn't had a chance to call yet." Angela wiped the sweat from her forehead. "I was the only one here; I had to call my cousin for help."

"Don't worry about it. I'm going to get her." He left and went to the dollar store, but there was an out-to-lunch sign on the door.

****

"Bitch," Diamond said into the phone. "What the hell you mean she locked up?" Her friend, Jasmine, was on the line.

"Girl, that's what Angela told me when she was doing my hair. I know I should've been called you girl, but I was rushing for work, and Angela's fat ass wanna spend thirty minutes in the dollar store buying pies and shit. I'm sorry, girl."

She stopped putting the gloss on her toenails. "It's okay, girl. Let me call this jail and see what's up. Love you, bitch."

She dialed for the jail. "Fulton County Annex?"

"I need to know why my sister is there."

"What's her name?"

"Nae, N-a-e, Waters."

There was a moment of silence as the woman searched the database. She came back with, "We have no inmate here by that name, ma'am. She could've been picked up by one of the surrounding counties."

Diamond hung up and quickly dialed Ken's number, assuming he'd bonded her out already. Her excitement ran through her body like an electric current.

"Yes?" he answered.

"You talked to her yet?"

"Yea, she's fine. You'll see her soon."

He hung up.

She was no longer sure of Ken. She could no longer control herself. She kept thinking about her mother and the possibility of Nae gone too. She began to cry, fearing the worse, and her fear soon became anger. If she didn't hear from her soon, she had something in store for Ken.

CHAPTER 15

Ken was fed up with all the nonsense and the run-around he was receiving in regard to Nae's whereabouts. Now, he was pulling into Fulton County Jail's parking lot for the second time today. His phone rang as he found a parking space. It was the same number that J-Bo usually called from, and he just knew it was her.

"Babe, are you aiight?" he answered after pressing five.

"Da hell you talkin' bout, shawty?" J-Bo's voice came across the line.

"Damn, I'm trippin'. What's up, bro?"

"Aye, you memba da nigga we talked about earlier?"

Preoccupied with thoughts of Nae, It took him a moment to piece it together. "Yea, what about him?"

"It's just what I thought. They're brothers."

"How do you know?"

"I was talkin' to my lil side hoe. She was tellin' me 'bout a situation her cousin's boyfriend got goin on."

"Umm," Ken paused. "I want to know how I came in the picture."

"Ion know, shawty, but dat ain't important right now."

"You right. Anything else?"

"Nah, I had to finesse dat lil bitch. I ain't wanna ask too many questions."

"That's right." He was about to hang up, but he asked, "Your side piece; what's her cousin's name?"

"She a dancer, go by Ferrari, Ion know shawty's real name."

****

"How may I help you?" the fat deputy asked.

“Nae Waters,” Ken said. “What’s the charge and bond?”

“Let’s see.” The deputy’s pudgy fingers danced across the keyboard. “Did you say, Nae Waters?”

“Um-hmm.

Her fingers did another dance. She studied the monitor, then gazed at Ken. “Sir, we have no one in custody by that name.”

“Could you try it again, please?” he asked politely, aggravated.

She did, and this time she turned the monitor around for him to see: Nae wasn’t there.

“Try DeKalb or Clayton,” the deputy suggested.

But Ken had done that and more already and had come back again to Fulton. He'd called a few bondsmen as well, with every one of them claiming they have neither heard nor bonded anyone by that name.

Back behind the wheel, he sat processing it all. There was no way Nae could be in custody with no record of which. Ken considered the nigga in the Equinox, the threatening call to his office, and the fact the caller’s family name was tied to J-Bo’s case. Ken was beginning to suspect foul play, and confirmation of which appeared in the form of a text message to his phone.

Baby, it’s me; I was kidnapped. I don’t know where I am. They said they would kill me if you didn’t come and meet them.

Baby, where am I supposed to meet them? Ken texted back.

The pink store in Pittsburgh, came Nae’s reply, *tonight at 10. They said to come alone.*

****

Mike smiled. “You gotta stupid ass boyfriend, shawty.” He held the phone in front of her face, showing her the text exchange between him and Ken. “Come on,” he laughed. “We got to get you all dressed to meet the nigga.”

The girls were given their clothes back. Afterwards, their hands were cuffed in front. “Please,” Nae sobbed as Mike snapped the cuffs to her wrists. “I never knew about your loss.”

He snatched her by the neck. “My lil brother was only seventeen,” he growled, squeezing tight. “So, I don’t give a fuck about you. I’ma kill both of you hoes and that nigga!” He held her neck a second longer before releasing his grip, glaring as she panted for breath.

Tisha wanted to protest, but remained fearfully silent, crying quietly.

“What the hell you cryin’ foe?” Mike came to where she sat on the mattress. He unbuttoned his pants to expose his flaccid penis. She understood the implication but stared defiantly at him.

Mike retrieved the pistol from where it lay on the chair, returned to Tisha, then pointed the pistol at Nae. “Do it,” he threatened, “or I’ll put one in the bitch. And if your teeth so much as scrape my shit, I’ma put one in you- and her for the fuck of it.”

Nae looked apologetically at Tisha as she took Mike’s pen is into her mouth. The girl was afraid, and her performance was a piss poor one, not that it should have been anything but, considering the circumstances. However, it wasn’t long before he pulled out and nutted on her face.

“Now you,” he told Nae, “Come lick it off.”

“Please,” Nae cried.

“Please, what, bitch?” He raised the gun threateningly at Tisha. “Get yo ass over here and lick this shit off!”

Nae leaned towards her friend and licked her tear-streaked and semen-covered face. It was degusting to the point she quivered from the taste.

"Swallow it," Mike demanded.

"Pleeease," Nae hummed, wanting desperately to spit it out.

Mike raised the pistol threateningly.

"Okay!" she relented, swallowing the rancid fluid. The semen slid down her throat- and came right back up, followed by puke.

Mike stepped back, leaped clear to be missed by the vomit, and flipped his dick back in his pants. "Nasty ass bitch," he mumbled.

****

As usual, Chingy was at the dining room table counting money and smoking a blunt when Ken put in his appearance. "What's good?" Chingy greeted.

"Lily got back with you?" Ken sat down and got straight to the point.

Lily was a friend of Ken's. They went to high school together, and Ken had always looked at her like a sister. At some point, she'd gotten into prostitution and had become a drug addict. Ken, feeling some type of way about her downwards spiral, intervened with the necessary emotional and financial support to get her cleaned up. He sent her to rehab. Thereafter, he pulled strings, and with a little money, he got her hired with the DMV. With that, of course, she never hesitated to provide intel on any specific person, as was the case now.

"Yeah," Chingy said, pulling on his blunt, inhaling deep." It's a Cobb County address. Ariel Rogers. She's sixty, so it gotta be mama or grandmamma. I got it all written down."

"Alright," Ken said. "I'm gone make a very long story short. I've been getting followed. My lady got snatched last night. It's a clown-ass nigga named Mike that's behind it. His lil brother is the young nigga that J-Bo and Flip took out. I don't know how he linked me to them, but it is what it is." He took a deep breath.

"Shid, we got his ass now," Chingy said.

"Hopefully. We're not one hundred percent sure. Get some young niggas and strap up." Ken stood to his feet and dapped Chingy up. "Young Boss, Young Boss."

Chingy nodded. "25-2, I'll never cross."

****

Flip was crushing up sixty packs of noodles on the floor, emptying the contents in a big trash bag. One of the guys downstairs was doing the same thing with sixty more. Flip added twenty bags of refried beans and thirty bags of jalapeno Cheetos. They were served pizza for dinner, and he made everybody scrape off their meat and cheese to contribute to the meal.

Everybody was doing something. Most of the guys were chopping up pickles and pouring the pickle juice into the bottles of squeeze cheese to loosen it up so it would be enough for everybody to get an even share.

J-Bo was in another room making the cakes. He had fifty iced honey buns, thirty packs of Swiss Rolls, thirty boxes of Buddy Bars, ten jars of peanut butter, and ten jars of chocolate mixing that they bought from one of the guys that worked in the kitchen. Both dorm's ice coolers were filled with Bombay. Nigga felt like it was their birthday in that bitch!

"I hope y'all niggas don't neva get out!" one of the guys joked.

"Nigga fuck you!" Flip shot back. Even though they were just bullshitting, some people didn't want them to go for real.

"Y'all boys wanna go to the club?" J-Bo asked.

"Hell yea!" they roared.

"Hit that shit, Psycho!"

Psycho was the hottest thing since Lil Dread, and J-Bo promised him a record deal with YoungBoss when he got out.

Someone started making a beat on the table, vocalizing a corresponding melody to go with it. Psycho caught the rhythm and started to ride:

"I'ma solid nigga, drinkin' up codeine and smokin' weed that's me boy! Nigga keep talkin' dumb grab dat mothafuckin choppa cut thru ya stomach like a breach, boy! I know a lot of y'all niggas fake. That's why I gotta keep my heat, boy. Heard them suckas say that they want beef, so I'm grindin' my teeth wit my hand on my heat, boy!" he tongue twisted.

They all cheered and sung along for the ones that knew the song. They all poured their Bombay and made a toast. Psycho stood on the table, holding his cup high. "To my niggas gettin' freed up." They recited before touching cups.

J-Bo looked at his little cousin, feeling emotional. They just wagged three bodies. And knowing the possibility of having to spend the rest of their life behind bars, neither once considered turning on the other for a lesser sentence. J-Bo hugged Flip. "I love you, lil cuz."

"I love you too, my nigga."

"Hold up! Y'all niggas bet not start all that sensitive ass shit."

The cousins started boxing and wrestling with Psycho. If it was a real fight, they would have been fucking Psycho up.

Everybody put their cups down and joined the fight. They looked like a bunch of big ass kids at Chuck E cheese

"Ninedy's!" one of the ninety babies yelled, and they all started attacking the older niggas.

CHAPTER 16

They rode through the windy night five deep in a white Hummer H3. Chingy had one of the young niggas steal a license plate from another Hummer of the same model, so a reported tag wouldn't link to them. They couldn't risk the same thing that transpired with J-Bo and Flip happening to them.

"Alright, listen," Ken said, turning right off the Thornton Road exit. He set fire to a plastic-tipped Black & Mild, took a pull, and exhaled. "Hopefully, this nigga is here." He turned right again on Maxham Road as the GPS instructed. "Peanut and Smoke?" He looked at them through his rear-view mirror. "I hope y'all lil niggas ready."

"Old lady. Lil Baby," Seventeen-year-old Peanut shot back. "I don't give no fuck. I'ma hitta."

"Fuckin' right." Smoke added, cocking his pistol.

Ken passed the Black to Chingy in the passenger seat, who puffed a few times before passing it to Smoke. Tez had sent the two youngins on a mission a few years ago. They succeeded. He took them to Chingy, vouched for them, and they soon had his approval, officially stamped with YoungBoss. Ken liked the fact they listened and paid attention to every word. There was nothing better than a soldier that paid attention.

"There will be no shooting going down tonight," Ken stressed. "Unless you're put in a life-or-death situation." He looked at everybody for their understanding. They all nodded.

Their route took them through a school district.

"Oh, shit!" Smoke said, pointing to South Cobb High School as they passed. Ken turned left on Clay Road. "I be fuckin' a lil hoe dat go there."

"Her name bet not be Jasmine," Peanut said.

"Dark skin, long hair with dimples?" Smoke asked.

Peanut's eyes grew wide. "Aw, hell naw!"

They all laughed.

"Damn, Peanut," Tez teased. "He fuckin' yo hoe."

They were laughing and kicking the shit but would get serious in the blink of an eye. Killing was nothing to them. It's who they were, what they did.

"Alright," Ken caught everyone's attention. "Who wanna stay in the car?"

It was the question they all dreaded; everyone wanted a piece of the action.

Ken made a left turn on Flint Hill Road and took the first right into The Village subdivision, nicknamed Blue Village because it was a known Crip territory.

"So," Ken grabbed the Black from Tez and pulled hard. "Aint nobody heard me?" He parked in front of a grey house. No one had yet to speak. "Tez? You stay," Ken decided. "Keep this bitch running."

Tez sucked his teeth. "C'mon, big bruh. Why I gotta stay?"

"Because I know how you rock. I wanna see bout the other two." He nodded towards Peanut and Smoke. He'd sent them on missions through Tez or Chingy over the years, but this was the first time they actually done anything with him.

"Man aiight."

Tez looked at all the houses, not understanding how this was a gang area. All the lawns were nicely mowed, pretty flowers were planted, and neat little birdhouses were in almost every yard.

"Let's make this shit quick." Ken pulled the white mask over his face. The others followed suit. "Peanut, go through the back with Chingy. Smoke, come with me through the front." He peered around for nosey neighbors or any potential threats, finding there was none. Tez was in the driver's seat the moment Ken's feet touched the ground. Peanut and Chingy jumped the fence leading to the backyard.

"Fuck!" Tez slapped the wheel.

****

"Promise me you're going to make it over for dinner, baby," Ariel spoke to her grandson on the phone.

"I promise, Ma. I just gotta handle something with Pops real quick. We gone be there." He looked at his watch—9 pm.

"Okay, baby," she hung up.

Ariel was a black woman, in great shape to be sixty years of age, despite the wrinkling skin and gray hair. It was clear she took good care of herself in her youth.

In the kitchen, she opened the oven to check her baked chicken. In just a few moments, it would be ready for the broiler. The peach cobbler was nearly done. She rubbed her fingers on the soft fabric of the blue, flower covered apron. All was well, and everything would be ready by the time her son and grandson arrived. There was often-

A thunderous crash from the living room startled the older woman. She hurried towards the sound and ran right into Ken with his outstretched .45. A similar noise came from the rear of the house, and it was clear that, like her front door, her back door was kicked in.

"Find him," Ken told his crew as Peanut and Chingy met with them in the living room.

"Where is Mike?" he asked Ariel.

Fear incapacitated the woman, and for a second, she couldn't speak. "He- he doesn't live here," she finally managed to get out.

Ken gestured towards the small sofa near a Cherry wood coffee table. "Have a seat," he said. "I want Mike's phone number and his address. Give me the wrong information, and you will regret it."

****

"Tisha, I am so sorry, girl," Nae offered a sincere apology. First, she had got her pistol-whipped, now this.

"Girl, stop that shit," Tisha said.

"But what if we don't make it out alive?" It was a concept Nae didn't want to consider, but a reality they faced.

"Then, that just means it's our time to go, Nae." She paused. "Girl, did you know this nigga was involved in all this crazy street shit?"

"Girl, no," Nae admitted. "But I don't think that would have changed me fucking with him if I had an idea."

Tisha believed her. She bumped Nae's shoulder, and they both smiled.

"Come on, girl, let's pray," Nae suggested. They both bowed their heads. "God, please, have mercy on our souls if we die tonight. Please protect us, protect Diamond and Ken too, Father God. Protect Tisha's family too, Father God." She paused, thinking of what more to say.

"Bitch, I'm God!" Mike interrupted. "You should be praying to me." Neither of them had heard him come in. "Y'all cute," he said." I'll make sho' we have a threesome before I kill you both."

Pops entered and asked, "They ready?"

Mike checked the time on Nae's phone, and almost on cue, there were knocks at the front door. Pops left and returned with two young men dressed in dark blue.

"Y'all park across the street from the pink store. I'ma direct him out the car from here," he said, holding up Nae's phone. "I want his ass alive, but if he tries anything slick, you know what to do."

Pops didn't object. He allowed Mike to think he was running the show because he wanted Ken first. He was going to gun him down whether he tried something slick or not.

****

"Yea, that's the house," Ken said, driving past a small house on Smith Street.

"You sho'?" Tez asked from the passenger seat.

Ken nodded as he looked hard at the black equinox parked in the driveway. The plate number was the same as the one he'd spotted earlier with the woman behind the wheel. As bad as he wanted to kill Mike by himself, Ken allowed Tez to roll shotgun because he stayed in the car the last time.

His phone rang. "Hey, baby, What's up?"

"Ken, where are you?"

He could tell she was pressured to speak. "Listen, baby, you and your friend are good. Don't worry about shit; I got you."

His confidence brought a smile to her lips.

Mike snatched the phone from her. "Where da fuck you at nigga? You betta pull up to da pink store before I kill these hoes!" he wolfed.

"You do know I know who you are, right?"

Mike wasn't buying that shit. "Yea, I'm the boogie man bitch-"

Ken ended the call before he could continue.

"Oh, dis nigga must don't love you," he murmured to Nae, redialing Ken's number from Nae's phone, receiving no answer. He made a second attempt but ended the call when his own phone rang. He knew it was Pops, so he answered quickly, without checking the caller ID. "Oh, wassup, Pops?"

"How you feeling tonight, Michael?" It was Ken on the line.

"Pops!" Mike's voice was laced with panic.

"Don't call daddy now, nigga. Let me speak to my lady."

"Nigga, fuck that hoe! Come to the pink store, or she dies now."

"I don't think you wanna do that, Michael." His calm sent chills through Mike's veins.

Having forced Mike's grandma to give up her grandson's number and address, Ken had sat a few houses down from the spot, patiently waiting and watching, and was rewarded with Pops leaving the house with two goons. He waited a few moments longer to be sure all was as it seemed to be before he and Tez left the vehicle and crept toward the small house.

"Nigga, you think I'm playing? I gotta show you I'm serious?" He pointed his weapon at Nae's leg, and she cried out.

"Ok, ok," Ken said. "Before you do that, I have someone for you to talk to." Ken was on a three-way call with Chingy, who was with Ariel. On cue, she was placed on the line.

"Michael, sweetie," she cried. "Please do what they say."

Mike's heart sank. "Mama!" he screamed, feeling his whole world crashing down.

"Now, fuck nigga," Ken said, creeping silently onto Mike's front porch. "If you lay a finger on her, it's over with for the old bitch. She and the rest of your family." He twisted the doorknob to the front door and found it locked. He signaled Tez, and they crept around to the side door.

"Mike," Ken demanded. "Let the women go, now. Free them from wherever they are."

"Aiight bruh, they walkin' out now." In that moment, Mike regretted his every move, understanding the true caliber of nigga he was fucking with. He un-cuffed the women as a few tears trickled from his eyes.

The side door was locked. With that being the case, Ken and Tez crept back to the front door and knelt under the big windows.

"Okay," Mike said. "I'm sendin' dem out now." He directed them to the living room, where he followed, peeping cautiously out the window. He was on high alert, eyes sweeping up and down the block in search of anything out of place. In his mind, if they could find his mother, they could very much be lurking around in the dark. Seeing nothing out of the ordinary, he opened the door and let Nae and Tisha out. "Shawty," Mike said desperately. "They goin' out now. Where my mama?"

Just as Mike was reaching to close the door after the women, Tez sprang to his feet and shoved his 9mm in Mike's face, startling the girls on the porch and pushing the man back inside the house. Mike's tears ran freely now, with the understanding that his fate would be something similar to what he'd had in store for Ken and the girls.

"All secure," Ken said to Chingy, who was still on the line. In route in five." Ken touched the Bluetooth earpiece to end the call, then Nae became the center of his attention. He turned to her, and she rushed into his arms. "Damn, baby girl, I'm sorry." He attempted to kiss, but she pulled back. Ken's brow creased in confusion.

"Not now, Ken. Just… Please." Nae turned her head and dropped her gaze. She wanted nothing more than to kiss her man passionately, but there was no way she was going to kiss him after swallowing another man's cum. She couldn't disrespect him like that.

"Bae?" Ken started to protest, thinking she was worried about her breath, but let it go at the defeated look on her face. He turned to Tisha, "I apologize to you, too."

Nae and Tisha were dirty, their hair disheveled. You could tell they had been roughed up, and their red-rimmed eyes made it evident that they had been crying non-stop. Ken was tempted to kill Mike on the spot but seeing Tisha's black eye and the distress on both women's tear-streaked faces. He decided not to do it just yet. In just a few seconds, they had Mike's wrists locked behind his back with the same cuffs he had used to restrain Nae and Tisha. They hustled to the Hummer, where Ken took the wheel, with Nae beside him in the passenger seat. Tisha sat behind Nae, and Tez sat behind Ken with Mike beside him at gunpoint.

"Which one of you punk ass niggas punched Nae in her stomach," Ken asked the second they were on the move.

"It was Skip," Mike was quick to answer.

"He one of them niggas at the pink store?" Ken asked.

"Yeah," Mike said.

Ken nodded.

They arrived at the pink store to find the same three males Ken had observed leaving Pops' place, posted near a truck. The Equinox. Ken rolled down the window. "Yo Pops!" he called out. "Me and Mike got some understandin'. He told me to come here and drop this money off to Skip!"

Skip looked at Pops, and Pops nodded.

The dumbfounded boy approached the truck with confidence. Before his brain could process what was going on, Ken stuck his arm out the window and let loose with his .45. The explosions were loud in the night, the fire coming from the barrel bright. Four slugs tore through Skip's body, and a fifth one took him in the head. Before his body hit the ground, Ken sent the remainder of his slugs at the other two, who were taken by surprise and already under fire from Tez's 9mm.

Mike closed his eyes. Both Nae and Tisha were screaming. Tez was still shooting as he backed up to the Hummer's open door. He jumped back inside, and Ken smashed off, speeding towards Dill Avenue.

CHAPTER 17

Chingy was standing in the furniture-less living room of the dark bando with Takia aimed at the front door as it swung open. Recognizing his homies, Ken and Tez, he lowered the weapon. He noted the two rescued women and the cuffed male with them.

"Dis da lil pussy-ass nigga?" Chingy said, sizing Mike up.

"Yea," Ken nodded, a firm grip on Mike's arm, half shoving, half dragging the nigga to one of the back rooms. The others followed.

Ariel was on the hardwood floor, hands tied in the front with a thick cord. Smoke and Peanut sat her up to greet the newcomers. Mike, terrified of the worse, mentally cursed himself for dismissing his Pops' suggestion to leave it all alone. Instead, he'd forced the man's hand. Pops was dead as a result, and from the looks of it all, he and his grandma would soon suffer a similar fate.

"Baby," Ken turned to Nae. "What did he do to you, baby?"

Nae looked to Tisha, and they began to cry, glad to be free from their recent captors, yet terribly shaken by what had happed and what was unfolding before them, having no prior experience with the likes of which. Their tears angered Ken, who turned and struck Mike in the jaw with a hard right, knocking him to the floor next to Ariel.

Ken took Nae's trembling hands. "Nae, what did he do to you, love?"

"He demoralized me. He said he was going to fuck us both before killing us. He hit Tisha and made her suck his little dick," her voice broke, and there was a second before she could go on. "Then he made me lick his cum off her face and swallow." She gagged and emptied the contents of her stomach on the hardwood floor, some of which splashed on Ken's boot.

Ken kissed her forehead when she recovered. "Say no more." He looked down at Mike. "So, you made my lady lick some fucking cum?" He clenched his fist. "Cool." He nodded to Ariel. "Untie her."

Peanut moved to comply.

"Anybody wants some head from this old bitch?" Ken asked.

All the fellas shook their heads, no.

"How about y'all?" he asked the ladies.

They declined with screwed faces.

"So, you mean to tell me," he glanced around the room, "don't nobody in this mothafucka want head from this old bitch?" He knelt, caressing Ariel's face.

"Please, bruh," Mike pleaded. "I let ya girls go. Let my grandma go."

Smoke delivered a vicious kick to Mike's stomach. "You ain't had a choice, nigga. Shut da fuck up!"

Ken pointed at Ariel and then to Mike. "You gon' suck his dick."

Mike's stomach turned at the idea.

Ken instructed Smoke and Peanut to pull Mike's pants down.

"Sir," she pleaded. "Please don't make me do this. He is my grandbaby."

Chingy stood over the woman and slapped her hard across the face. "Shut da fuck up."

"He's gonna die regardless," Ken told the older woman. "But if you comply, you might live. Now take your clothes off. I'm sure he would rather see you naked while you blow him off."

Ariel stared Ken hard in the eyes. It was clear she didn't believe him, but what choice did she have? With that being the case, she stripped herself naked, crawled over to Mike, and took hold of his flaccid penis. She hesitated, then with tears streaming down her face, she took him into her mouth.

There was a collective gasp from the women. Nae couldn't believe what was taking place before her eyes. She was appalled, yet she did not turn away, compelled to watch.

"Bitch, moan," Tez commanded. "Let him know you enjoying yourself."

Peanut's Timberland boot crashed into the side of Mike's head. "You too, fuck nigga!"

Mike's cry from the blow became a continuous moan.

"Let me know when you 'bout to cum," Ken threatened. "If you don't, I'm gonna personally put one in this old bitch's dome."

The seconds ticked away. Aside from the couple's forced moans and Ariel's smacking performance, all was silent; no one spoke.

"Ah!" Mike cried, "Gra'ma, get off!"

"Stand his bitch ass up!" Ken commanded, directing Peanut and Tez to act. "You," he pointed at Ariel. "Lay back and catch it all between your legs."

Ariel, humiliated and crying silently, fell back on her elbows with knees drawn and legs parted receptively as Peanut and Tez snatched Mike to his feet.

Cuffed as he was and unable to direct the flow, Mike's semen shot forward, hitting the floor, Ariel's stomach as well as the shaved folds of her vagina.

"Now, get yo bitch ass on yo knees and lick it off," Ken ordered.

Mike dropped to his knees and licked his own semen off Ariel's stomach.

"Swallow it," Ken commanded.

Mike did as was told, then made an attempt to put some distance between him and Ariel, but he was halted by Ken's second command.

"Get the rest of it!"

Mike's expression was incredulous. "Man, that's all of it."

"No, the fuck it ain't!" Ken pointed to the semen on Ariel's vaginal lips. "Nigga get that too."

"Man, I-" *umfffffph!*

Mike's protest was cut off by a kick in the ribs from Peanut. "Nigga, you heard what the fuck he said!"

With every bit of reluctance one should have for such an occasion, Mike lowered his head between Ariel's legs and did what he was told.

"Aw!" the exclamation came from Nae.

Tisha made a sound in the back of her throat.

Ariel, crying silently up until this point, verbalized her distaste with the matter. "Oh my God, no!"

"Bitch, shut the fuck up!" Ken said, pointing the .45 at her head. "Don't close your legs, and you bet' not move!"

Mike was thorough with licking it up, wanting it all over and done. He raised his head, swallowed, and fell away from Ariel. "Bruh," he pleaded. "Can you please let her go now?"

"She can go when I say she can go." Ken raised his boot to Ariel's face." Lick it off." He referred to Nae's puke that had gotten on his feet.

She did as she was told.

"And while you're at it," Ken gestured toward the semen on the floor. "Go ahead and get what your grandson left for you."

As Ariel went about licking her grandson's semen from the floor, Ken nodded to Peanut before giving his attention to Tisha and Nae. He put an arm around each, turning their backs on the scene. "Never repeat the events of this night," he whispered to them. "Not ever. Understand?"

They both nodded.

Ken glanced over his shoulder at Ariel. She was done licking the floor, curled now into a ball. Her body racked with silent convulsions. "Okay," he said to her. "Now you can go."

At that, Peanut housed a single round into the back of Ariel's head.

Mike choked on his scream.

"And you can go with her," Smoke said, dumping two rounds into Mike's skull, silencing his choking sobs.

"Let's ride," Ken ordered. He took Nae's hand, and with her free hand, she took Tisha's. Ken was proud of the team he'd put together. He couldn't wait for the moment J-Bo and Flip were free; a major celebration was in order.

Gunfire erupted from the street the moment they set foot on the porch.

"Oh, shit!" Ken pushed Nae to the ground and fired back. Tisha, startled by the sudden exchange, threw up her hands as if she was fending off a physical attack.

Nae tried to pull her down, but the bullets were too fast. Tisha was struck several times before falling lifelessly to the porch.

"Noooo!" Nae cried.

Pinned under gunfire from three anonymous shooters, Chingy checked Takia's safety, and with a cry of, "Fuck dat shit!" he jumped to his feet and fired wildly. His bullets ripped through the night, punching holes through the driver's side door of a blue Pontiac G6 at the curb, penetrating the front wall and shattering the windows of the single-story house directly across from them. Holes were punched through two of the shooters as well. The first fell motionlessly to the ground, the second lay writhing in pain, having neglected his gun and clutching his chest.

The third shooter let off a few more rounds, one of which caught Chingy in the head.

"Oh, fuck no!" Tez shouted, coming to his feet as Chingy's body fell next to Ken.

The third shooter turned tail, and Tez was off the porch in hot pursuit. He slowed long enough to put the fallen shooter out of his misery with a bullet to his head. Tez shot twice the moment he got a clear line of sight. His aim was off, running as he was, shooting at a fleeing target. The shooter darted between a blue BMW and a grey Nissan Altima two and crossed to the far side of the street, racing up the sidewalk. Tez crossed over before reaching the BMW. He stopped suddenly on the sidewalk and fired twice again. The fleeing figure stumbled-hit once in the back – and fell to the ground, losing his gun in the process. Tez sprinted to catch up, even as the shooter scrambled to his feet to resume his desperate flight for life. Having closed some distance between them, Tez let loose two more shots, and both struck home, taking the fleeing figure to the ground for the second time. More damage done than before, the shooter wasn't as quick to rise, and with Tez coming at full speed, the shooter had barely gotten to one knee when he was kicked in the side of the head. The blow carried him onto his back, where he lay panting, bleeding from the mouth.

Tez stood over the fallen man; gun pointed at his head.

"Who da fuck is you, nigga?"

"Ugggh fuck!" the shooter said. He turned his head to one side and spat a mouth full of blood. "Y'all niggas tryna steal our blocks? We gone die bout dat shit, shawty!"

"What da fuck you talkin' bout?" Tez shot back.

"What da fuck was y'all doin' coming out our spot? All our work in there, nigga don't play stupid!"

"Nigga, we YoungBoss! We don't want y'all petty ass blocks!" Tez put two rounds in the man's head before running back to the bando.

Peanut and Smoke were situating Ken's motionless body in the back of the Hummer. If a brother dies in battle and the entire membership is pressed for time, that brother is left and later given a proper burial. It was protocol. With that, Ken had to be alive.

Nae was kneeling over Tisha's body and screaming hysterically when Tez reached her side. He snatched her by the arm. "She's gone, baby girl. I'm sorry, but we gotta go."

They stepped over Chingy's lifeless body and hurried to the Hummer where Tez helped her climb into the backseat beside a shallow breathing Ken, whose head rested in Smoke's lap. He was bleeding heavily from the torso. Tez hopped in the passenger seat, and police sirens could be heard from afar as Peanut took them away from the scene.

****

I can't believe this shit. Why God? Why me? Why do I gotta go through this? I obey you as best I can. Please just fix this, Nae prayed silently, standing behind a thick glass in the hospital's ER looking at Tisha's body lying on a steel table. By the time they dropped Ken off, the ambulance was arriving with Tisha and the other bodies.

"Ma'am, you can change out while you wait for the police." A nurse gave her a gown and offered to wash her bloody clothes.

****

Tez was parked in a white Avalanche at a mom and pops thrift store about two minutes down the street from the hospital. After getting Ken out, he had one of the homies come swap whips with him and bring clothes. He sent Peanut along to set that Hummer on fire.

"Shawty got four minutes." He looked at his G-shock. He told Nae she had twelve minutes to see Ken and Tisha's body one last time, and he was leaving with or without her. He wanted to go see the fellas one last time, but after dropping Ken off and swerving off the way he did, he knew that would bring way too many questions he wasn't ready to answer.

Smoke pulled the tank top over his head. "Shit kinda tight, huh?" Tez looked at him but never replied. Tez had sent their old clothes along with the truck to be burned. Just as he started the ignition, he saw Nae in his rearview mirror speed walking towards them. When she opened the door, he handed her an empty Kroger's bag.

"Hurry up, take dat shit off, put it in there, and let's ride," he ordered. She wanted to say "fuck no" about stripping naked and jumping in his truck, but she knew now just wasn't the time. She confirmed, and hopped in.

"Here." Without looking back, Smoke tossed her his white T that he was planning on wearing over his tank top.

She still couldn't believe Tisha had just died before her very eyes like that. She'd never seen shit like that before. She was nervous, confused, and scared all at once. She didn't even know Chingy, but her heart went soft for him too. The one question she badly wanted an answer to was, would Ken live or not?

She attempted to visit his room before she left the hospital, but he had already undergone surgery. She'd also overheard one of the nurses saying doing surgery on him would be pointless; it was clear to them that he was going to die regardless. She'd told Tez exactly what was said.

Time to boss up, he thought, mentally preparing himself for the responsibility. He knew being the big boss was a major responsibility and could be very stressful; especially, at his young age. Should age matter? He was born to be a boss, as long as he was ready for the punches that came with it.

"Right there." She pointed to the only car in the dark parking lot. She'd asked to be dropped off at the salon.

"You want me to follow you home, shawty?" Tez offered.

She shook her head no.

"Take my numba. Hit me if you need anything."

"I don't have my phone." She opened the door.

He fished through the glove compartment and found a pen and a few Zaxby's napkins and jotted his number down on it. When she grabbed the number, their fingers locked for a few seconds. They made eye contact. Tez quickly broke it, and she turned her back.

"Wait."

She turned around.

"You got yo keys, shawty?"

She shamefully dropped her head. "No, I got a spare in the shop, if you can help me get in."

He looked to Smoke, knowing he was good at shit like that. He used two pens from her hair and the ink pen that Tez had and had the door opened in forty seconds. She ran in to grab her key, stopped the alarm, and reset it.

"I can't lock it back," Smoke said when she returned.

"It's fine." Her voice was tired.

Tez could tell that she was stressed over the events of that night. He reminded her again that if she needed anything to hit his line, she promised she would. They said their goodbyes, goodnights and drove in opposite directions.

"So, Ken ain't gon' make it?" asked Tez.

CHAPTER 18
THREE DAYS LATER

Lil Dread, Tez, Peanut, Smoke, Nae, and fifty other YoungBoss members were standing outside. The sun was beaming down heavy, but there was a cool breeze that kept the balance. There was a beautiful Mother Nature smell of leaves, and as the preacher was saying his last words, Chingy's body was being lowered into the ground.

They laid Tisha's body the day before. Tez gave her $10,000 to ensure she could afford a decent casket along with a proper burial and shit. He had gone by all the spots and collected the money, one of Chingy's old jobs. Lil Dread paid $250,000 for an all-gold casket so Chingy could rest peacefully in. Once the pastor left, Tez stood beside the hole in the ground and placed his right hand over his heart; everyone followed suit, even Nae. She figured that's the way they showed respect.

"I pledge allegiance to all da bosses," they all repeated after him. "To every street nigga, every hood, every nation," as they all repeated after him, he realized he was staring into a pair of light, pretty brown eyes. She nervously broke eye contact, and that caused him to smile. "Rest in peace, Chingy. Rest in power, good brotha. We will finish what we started. YoungBoss, YoungBoss, 25-2 I'll neva cross." Everyone then bowed their heads for a sixty-second moment of silence, and then they parted ways. They had all agreed to link up later in ally for J-Bo and Flip's homecoming.

****

"Mr. Griffith is in a coma, and he's hooked up to a ventilator. His pulse is fifty beats per minute, which is extremely low and steady dropping, his blood pressure is eighty over sixty. This man took three bullets to his torso from a powerful weapon, Detective. He cannot move, talk, or breathe on his own, and I doubt he can hear us right now." The doctor quickly grew frustrated with the homicide detective. He'd been down to the hospital every day asking of Ken's condition so he could question him after the doctor had already told him he would call if he got any better.

"Any contacts for him?"

"No, Detective. I've already told you this twice. The people who dropped him off only told us that his name before driving off. But there was a woman that called this morning, her name Susie. She said he's her boss over some music group and said that she was his power of attorney, so I asked her to come down and take him off life support.

"How long do you give him to live, Doctor?"

"Forty-eight hours."

****

Holy shit! What the flick! How the fuck! When the fuck! This little cock-sucking son-of-a-bitch! I can't fucking believe this shit!

Mr. Luis' brain ached. He was seated beside J-Bo and Flip at trial. Realizing what was going on, J-Bo quickly wiped the falling tear from his eyes. Flip's face was unbending as if he was taking a hard shit.

"How is this possible?" J-Bo whispered. He reiterated his question, still receiving no answer.

"I-I-I don't know, Jerome. Your buddy says he paid one-hundred large."

J-Bo looked back in search of Ken with a pair of fiery eyes. He wasn't there. Shakeena and the baby were seated on the first row, and the rest of that side was YoungBoss members. Shakeena blew him a kiss when he looked back. But where was Ken? Lil Dread, Tez, Smoke, and Peanut came strutting inside the courtroom. Tez's arrogant smile quickly faded when he peeped the move. J-Bo knew something was terribly wrong.

Moments later, Nae came through the door.

What da fuck she doin here? Tez thought, meeting her gaze, she was equally baffled. Looking to J-Bo, she had a flashback. As many times as she had seen his face on the news and how familiar she thought he and Flip looked, it finally hit her. They'd attended the same high school.

Tez whispered something in Peanut's ear, and Peanut quickly turned and walked out. Diamond sat behind the stand, receiving cold stares from damn near everybody. She knew she was dead ass wrong for accepting the money and still proceeding with the testimony, but justice needed to be served. Plus, she really had assumed that Ken had hurt Nae.

If she knew the entire family that she wanted to serve justice to so bad were all dead, would she still feel the same way?

She smiled hard, seeing that Nae was good and alive, she actually thought about getting up without saying another word and leaving with Nae, but she didn't exercise that thought.

J-Bo felt betrayed. He wondered why Ken hadn't answered the phone the past few days. Diamond had honestly told the entire story of what she was doing out there that night and pointed out the two cousins.

"Have the jury reached its verdict?" the white, fat, bald-headed judge asked.

Mr. Luis was sweating bullets, knowing what was about to happen. He'd seen it too many times before.

"Your honor, we the jury find both Jerome and Phillip Dew, guilty of the triple homicide in question of John Rogers, Sharika Collins, and the unborn baby that was in Ms. Collins' stomach at the time of her death."

Those words pierced the hearts of every YoungBoss member. Mr. Luis dropped his head. Flip shed a few tears. When they saw Tez shed a tear, Lil Dread, Smoke, and all of the other members agreed to tear that courtroom up, including beating the DA's and judge asses, but Tez told them no before they could do it. The judge said sentencing wouldn't be until next week before going into his chambers.

Billy and William hugged, shook the juror's hands, and laughed as the two were taken out.

"Man, what da fuck typa shit dis is!" Tez spat to Mr. Luis the moment they were in the hallway. Mr. Luis calmly explained that Ken had already paid the girl not to testify. Tez then explained why Ken hadn't been answering, and it all made sense.

****

ONE WEEK LATER…

J-Bo and Flip were sentenced to life in prison without the possibility of parole. Every YoungBoss member took that hard.

Tez spoke to J-Bo and Flip one time at a ten-minute visit that was permitted before he was put on administrative lockdown until the department of corrections came to pick them up. Mr. Luis ensured Tez that with the $4 million he paid to bribe the appeal judges and staff that the two cousins would win an appeal and be granted time served after a decade.

Tez had to put pressure on Susie to make her sign Ken's money over to him. She gladly did it in the name of wanting to keep her life. The cousins felt a little better. Tez promised to hold them down every day until they were released. J-Bo made him promise to do one more thing, but Tez ensured him that he was already on it.

****

TWO WEEKS LATER…

They were parked outside of a gated apartment complex on Thornton Road. It was a windy night, and the hard rain beat up the windows on Tez's black 2018 Escalade. They had to wait for someone to type in their resident's code so they could tailgate. It was a quiet neighborhood in Douglassville

Peanut had left the trial early to lurk in the parking lot for Diamond and had been following her around since that day. It was clear that once the state released her from their protection, this is the place she moved to. His truck almost got swiped by the gate as he shot in quickly behind a slow-moving ass Buick Century. He parked in front of the 2100 building.

"It's dat one." Peanut pointed to the apartment on the top right. He slid on his leather gloves and cocked back his nine. Tez carried a 44 bulldog. They were both dressed in black just like last time. This time they wore no mask.

"We don't shoot to injure," Tez said.

"We shoot to kill," Peanut completed the sentence.

****

Diamond lay in their queen-sized bed, so happy to be where she was. It wasn't the suburbs, but it was much better than where they'd come from. She only sported a green lace thong, her fine ass looking like a model. Her small titties were perfectly rounded. R. Kelly's *Black Panties* album played loudly as Garrett stood over her and undressed.

****

Nae stood in the shower, allowing the hot water to wash away all of her pain and tears. She'd been to the hospital every day to check on Ken. His condition was the same. Even though he lived beyond those forty-eight hours estimated by the doctor, it was clear that he was going to die. After he saved her life that night, she felt obligated to be there with him every step of the way.

She and Angela had just shut the salon down and were in the process of moving it to Austell. The new building was bigger, and she felt business would be bigger than ever. She still didn't know what Tez and the gang were doing in the courtroom that day. If they hadn't left so soon, she would have asked him in person. Now, every time she called, his phone went straight to voicemail.

****

"Dey might not hear dis," Tez said because of the heavy rain and the loud music from the other side of the door. At the same time, he and Peanut kicked the steel door with all their might, and like magic, it swung open. They entered quickly with their weapons drawn, ready to peel a cap back. The living room was empty. They entered the dimly lit room and immediately saw Garrett. His back was towards them, and he was slow stroking Diamond.

Peanut turned the music up to its max and turned the light wheel all the way to the right, making the room very bright. The moment Garrett pulled out of her gushy pussy to look back, Peanut filled his chest with hot lead. His body jerked before falling beside her. She screamed and got silent when Tez shoved the bulldog in her face. "Get back in doggy style, bitch."

"Da fuck you doin, big bruh?" asked Peanut. Tez ignored.

As she bent over on her hands and knees, she got a good look at the two. She recognized them from the courtroom and knew exactly what they came to do. Tez popped an inch or so of the weapon into her loose vagina. "This fa my brothas."

Nae came running through the door butt naked, screaming at the top of her lungs, butcher's knife in hand. Before she could process anything, Peanut sent two shots her way. One hit the wall, and the other hit her face. Her body hit the ground, and he trained his weapon on her just in case she moved. Diamond screamed and tried to pull away from the gun. That's when Tez squeezed the trigger twice, blowing her vagina and ass open to the size of a golf ball. The other round ripped all the way through her body and tore her entire jawline off. He wiped his .44 off on the sheets before fleeing the scene.

TO BE CONTINUED…

Murda Was the Case 2

Coming Soon

Submission Guideline

Submit the first three chapters of your completed manuscript to ldpsubmissions@gmail.com, subject line: Your book's title. The manuscript must be in a .doc file and sent as an attachment. Document should be in Times New Roman, double spaced and in size 12 font. Also, provide your synopsis and full contact information. If sending multiple submissions, they must each be in a separate email.

Have a story but no way to send it electronically? You can still submit to LDP/Ca$h Presents. Send in the first three chapters, written or typed, of your completed manuscript to:

LDP: Submissions Dept
Po Box 944
Stockbridge, Ga 30281

DO NOT send original manuscript. Must be a duplicate.

Provide your synopsis and a cover letter containing your full contact information.

Thanks for considering LDP and Ca$h Presents.

NEW RELEASES

FRIEND OR FOE 3 by MIMI
A GANGSTA'S KARMA by FLAME
NIGHTMARE ON SILENT AVE by CHRIS GREEN
THE STREETS MADE ME 3 by LARRY D. WRIGHT
MOBBED UP 3 by KING RIO
JACK BOYZ N DA BRONX 3 by ROMELL TUKES
A DOPE BOY'S QUEEN 3 by ARYANNA
MOB TIES 3 by SAYNOMORE
CONFESSIONS OF A GANGSTA by NICHOLAS LOCK
MURDA WAS THE CASE by ELIJAH R. FREEMAN

Coming Soon from Lock Down Publications/Ca$h Presents

BLOOD OF A BOSS **VI**

SHADOWS OF THE GAME II

TRAP BASTARD II

By **Askari**

LOYAL TO THE GAME **IV**

By **T.J. & Jelissa**

IF TRUE SAVAGE **VIII**

MIDNIGHT CARTEL IV

DOPE BOY MAGIC IV

CITY OF KINGZ III

NIGHTMARE ON SILENT AVE II

By **Chris Green**

BLAST FOR ME **III**

A SAVAGE DOPEBOY III

CUTTHROAT MAFIA III

DUFFLE BAG CARTEL VII

HEARTLESS GOON VI

By **Ghost**

A HUSTLER'S DECEIT III

KILL ZONE II

BAE BELONGS TO ME III

By **Aryanna**

COKE KINGS V

KING OF THE TRAP III

By **T.J. Edwards**

GORILLAZ IN THE BAY V

3X KRAZY III

De'Kari

KINGPIN KILLAZ IV

STREET KINGS III

PAID IN BLOOD III

CARTEL KILLAZ IV

DOPE GODS III

Hood Rich

SINS OF A HUSTLA II

ASAD

RICH $AVAGE II

By Troublesome

YAYO V

Bred In The Game 2

S. Allen

CREAM III

By Yolanda Moore

SON OF A DOPE FIEND III

HEAVEN GOT A GHETTO II

By Renta

LOYALTY AIN'T PROMISED III

By Keith Williams

I'M NOTHING WITHOUT HIS LOVE II

SINS OF A THUG II

TO THE THUG I LOVED BEFORE II

By Monet Dragun

QUIET MONEY IV

EXTENDED CLIP III

THUG LIFE IV

By **Trai'Quan**

THE STREETS MADE ME IV

By **Larry D. Wright**

IF YOU CROSS ME ONCE II

By **Anthony Fields**

THE STREETS WILL NEVER CLOSE II

By K'ajji

HARD AND RUTHLESS III

THE BILLIONAIRE BENTLEYS II

Von Diesel

KILLA KOUNTY II

By Khufu

MOBBED UP IV

By King Rio

MONEY GAME II

By Smoove Dolla

A GANGSTA'S KARMA II

By FLAME

JACK BOYZ VERSUS DOPE BOYZ

By Romell Tukes

MOB TIES IV

By SayNoMore

MURDA WAS THE CASE II

Elijah R. Freeman

Available Now

RESTRAINING ORDER **I & II**

By **CA$H & Coffee**

LOVE KNOWS NO BOUNDARIES **I II & III**

By **Coffee**

RAISED AS A GOON I, II, III & IV

BRED BY THE SLUMS I, II, III

BLAST FOR ME I & II

ROTTEN TO THE CORE I II III

A BRONX TALE I, II, III

DUFFLE BAG CARTEL I II III IV V VI

HEARTLESS GOON I II III IV V

A SAVAGE DOPEBOY I II

DRUG LORDS I II III

CUTTHROAT MAFIA I II

KING OF THE TRENCHES

By **Ghost**

LAY IT DOWN **I & II**

LAST OF A DYING BREED I II

BLOOD STAINS OF A SHOTTA I & II III

By **Jamaica**

LOYAL TO THE GAME I II III

LIFE OF SIN I, II III

By **TJ & Jelissa**

BLOODY COMMAS I & II

SKI MASK CARTEL I II & III

KING OF NEW YORK I II,III IV V

RISE TO POWER I II III

COKE KINGS I II III IV

BORN HEARTLESS I II III IV

KING OF THE TRAP I II

By **T.J. Edwards**

IF LOVING HIM IS WRONG…I & II

LOVE ME EVEN WHEN IT HURTS I II III

By **Jelissa**

WHEN THE STREETS CLAP BACK I & II III

THE HEART OF A SAVAGE I II III

By **Jibril Williams**

A DISTINGUISHED THUG STOLE MY HEART I II & III

LOVE SHOULDN'T HURT I II III IV

RENEGADE BOYS I II III IV

PAID IN KARMA I II III

SAVAGE STORMS I II

AN UNFORESEEN LOVE

By **Meesha**

A GANGSTER'S CODE I &, II III

A GANGSTER'S SYN I II III

THE SAVAGE LIFE I II III

CHAINED TO THE STREETS I II III

BLOOD ON THE MONEY I II III

By J-Blunt

PUSH IT TO THE LIMIT

By **Bre' Hayes**

BLOOD OF A BOSS **I, II, III, IV, V**

SHADOWS OF THE GAME

TRAP BASTARD

By **Askari**

THE STREETS BLEED MURDER **I, II & III**

THE HEART OF A GANGSTA I II& III

By **Jerry Jackson**

CUM FOR ME I II III IV V VI VII

An **LDP Erotica Collaboration**

BRIDE OF A HUSTLA **I II & II**

THE FETTI GIRLS **I, II& III**

CORRUPTED BY A GANGSTA I, II III, IV

BLINDED BY HIS LOVE

THE PRICE YOU PAY FOR LOVE I, II ,III

DOPE GIRL MAGIC I II III

By **Destiny Skai**

WHEN A GOOD GIRL GOES BAD

By **Adrienne**

THE COST OF LOYALTY I II III

By Kweli

A GANGSTER'S REVENGE **I II III & IV**

THE BOSS MAN'S DAUGHTERS I II III IV V

A SAVAGE LOVE **I & II**

BAE BELONGS TO ME I II

A HUSTLER'S DECEIT I, II, III

WHAT BAD BITCHES DO I, II, III

SOUL OF A MONSTER I II III

KILL ZONE

A DOPE BOY'S QUEEN I II III

By **Aryanna**

A KINGPIN'S AMBITON

A KINGPIN'S AMBITION **II**

I MURDER FOR THE DOUGH

By **Ambitious**

TRUE SAVAGE I II III IV V VI VII

DOPE BOY MAGIC I, II, III

MIDNIGHT CARTEL I II III

CITY OF KINGZ I II

NIGHTMARE ON SILENT AVE

By **Chris Green**

A DOPEBOY'S PRAYER

By **Eddie "Wolf" Lee**

THE KING CARTEL **I, II & III**

By **Frank Gresham**

THESE NIGGAS AIN'T LOYAL **I, II & III**

By **Nikki Tee**

GANGSTA SHYT **I II &III**

By **CATO**

THE ULTIMATE BETRAYAL

By **Phoenix**

BOSS'N UP **I , II & III**

By **Royal Nicole**

I LOVE YOU TO DEATH

By **Destiny J**

I RIDE FOR MY HITTA

I STILL RIDE FOR MY HITTA

By **Misty Holt**

LOVE & CHASIN' PAPER

By **Qay Crockett**

TO DIE IN VAIN

SINS OF A HUSTLA

By **ASAD**

BROOKLYN HUSTLAZ

By **Boogsy Morina**

BROOKLYN ON LOCK I & II

By **Sonovia**

GANGSTA CITY

By **Teddy Duke**

A DRUG KING AND HIS DIAMOND I & II III

A DOPEMAN'S RICHES

HER MAN, MINE'S TOO I, II

CASH MONEY HO'S

THE WIFEY I USED TO BE I II

By Nicole Goosby

TRAPHOUSE KING **I II & III**

KINGPIN KILLAZ I II III

STREET KINGS I II

PAID IN BLOOD **I II**

CARTEL KILLAZ I II III

DOPE GODS I II

By **Hood Rich**

LIPSTICK KILLAH **I, II, III**

CRIME OF PASSION I II & III

FRIEND OR FOE I II III

By **Mimi**

STEADY MOBBN' **I, II, III**

THE STREETS STAINED MY SOUL I II

By **Marcellus Allen**

WHO SHOT YA **I, II, III**

SON OF A DOPE FIEND I II

HEAVEN GOT A GHETTO

Renta

GORILLAZ IN THE BAY **I II III IV**

TEARS OF A GANGSTA I II

3X KRAZY I II

DE'KARI

TRIGGADALE I II III

MURDA WAS THE CASE

Elijah R. Freeman

GOD BLESS THE TRAPPERS I, II, III

THESE SCANDALOUS STREETS I, II, III

FEAR MY GANGSTA I, II, III IV, V

THESE STREETS DON'T LOVE NOBODY I, II

BURY ME A G I, II, III, IV, V

A GANGSTA'S EMPIRE I, II, III, IV

THE DOPEMAN'S BODYGAURD I II

THE REALEST KILLAZ I II III

THE LAST OF THE OGS I II III

Tranay Adams

THE STREETS ARE CALLING

Duquie Wilson

MARRIED TO A BOSS I II III

By Destiny Skai & Chris Green

KINGZ OF THE GAME I II III IV V

Playa Ray

SLAUGHTER GANG I II III

RUTHLESS HEART I II III

By Willie Slaughter

FUK SHYT

By Blakk Diamond

DON'T F#CK WITH MY HEART I II

By Linnea

ADDICTED TO THE DRAMA I II III

IN THE ARM OF HIS BOSS II

By Jamila

YAYO I II III IV

A SHOOTER'S AMBITION I II

BRED IN THE GAME

By S. Allen

TRAP GOD I II III

RICH $AVAGE

By Troublesome

FOREVER GANGSTA

GLOCKS ON SATIN SHEETS I II

By Adrian Dulan

TOE TAGZ I II III

LEVELS TO THIS SHYT I II

By Ah'Million

KINGPIN DREAMS I II III

By Paper Boi Rari

CONFESSIONS OF A GANGSTA I II III IV

By Nicholas Lock

I'M NOTHING WITHOUT HIS LOVE

SINS OF A THUG

TO THE THUG I LOVED BEFORE

By Monet Dragun

CAUGHT UP IN THE LIFE I II III

By Robert Baptiste

NEW TO THE GAME I II III

MONEY, MURDER & MEMORIES I II III

By **Malik D. Rice**

LIFE OF A SAVAGE I II III

A GANGSTA'S QUR'AN I II III

MURDA SEASON I II III

GANGLAND CARTEL I II III

CHI'RAQ GANGSTAS I II III

KILLERS ON ELM STREET I II III

JACK BOYZ N DA BRONX I II III

A DOPEBOY'S DREAM

By **Romell Tukes**

LOYALTY AIN'T PROMISED I II

By Keith Williams

QUIET MONEY I II III

THUG LIFE I II III

EXTENDED CLIP I II

By **Trai'Quan**

THE STREETS MADE ME I II III

By **Larry D. Wright**

THE ULTIMATE SACRIFICE I, II, III, IV, V, VI

KHADIFI

IF YOU CROSS ME ONCE

ANGEL I II

IN THE BLINK OF AN EYE

By **Anthony Fields**

THE LIFE OF A HOOD STAR

By Ca$h & Rashia Wilson

THE STREETS WILL NEVER CLOSE

By K'ajji

CREAM I II

By Yolanda Moore

NIGHTMARES OF A HUSTLA I II III

By King Dream

CONCRETE KILLA I II

By Kingpen

HARD AND RUTHLESS I II

MOB TOWN 251

THE BILLIONAIRE BENTLEYS

By Von Diesel

GHOST MOB

Stilloan Robinson

MOB TIES I II III

By SayNoMore

BODYMORE MURDERLAND I II III

By Delmont Player

FOR THE LOVE OF A BOSS

By C. D. Blue

MOBBED UP I II III

By King Rio

KILLA KOUNTY

By Khufu

MONEY GAME

By Smoove Dolla

A GANGSTA'S KARMA

By FLAME

BOOKS BY LDP'S CEO, CA$H

TRUST IN NO MAN

TRUST IN NO MAN 2

TRUST IN NO MAN 3

BONDED BY BLOOD

SHORTY GOT A THUG

THUGS CRY

THUGS CRY 2

THUGS CRY 3

TRUST NO BITCH

TRUST NO BITCH 2

TRUST NO BITCH 3

TIL MY CASKET DROPS

RESTRAINING ORDER

RESTRAINING ORDER 2

IN LOVE WITH A CONVICT

LIFE OF A HOOD STAR